For Those Whom God Has Blessed *with* Fingers

by Ken Sparling

Pedlar Press | Toronto

ACKNOWLEDGEMENTS

The publisher wishes to thank the Canada Council for the
Arts and the Ontario Arts Council for their generous support
of our publishing program.

LIBRARY AND ARCHIVES CANADA CATALOGUING
IN PUBLICATION DATA

Sparling, Ken, 1959-
    For those whom God has blessed with fingers / Ken
Sparling.

ISBN 1-897141-03-3

    I. Title.
PS8587.P223F67 2005   C813'.54   C2005-903717-2

Edited for the Press by Derek McCormack

First Edition

COVER Dennis Geden, *Calling Blackbirds*, 1981
DESIGN Zab Design & Typography, Winnipeg

Printed in Canada

THE CANADA COUNCIL | LE CONSEIL DES ARTS
FOR THE ARTS | DU CANADA
SINCE 1957 | DEPUIS 1957

ONTARIO ARTS COUNCIL
CONSEIL DES ARTS DE L'ONTARIO

I was the guy who always wants to talk about his home in a country in Eastern Europe. Then I was a woman who spoke no English and held English-language newspapers in front of her as she travelled home each night from work on the subway and dreamed of her home on a continent I've never heard of (and there's only seven, I thought, but apparently I was wrong). Then I was the young girl who will die in a traffic accident at age thirteen, telling bystanders who try unsuccessfully to free her from the burning wreck: "I'm too young to die." (Apparently she won't be.) Then I was that guy with the bad voice that scares people. But I wasn't scared. I'm not brave. I drink coffee. I eat out many nights a week. I wash my underwear by hand. I have pictures of my wife and children at my desk, but I've never been married. I have trouble keeping a job. This scares people. I was never the boy at the train station who looked back like he could see me, but I still believe he was seeing what he wanted to see, so unless he wanted to see me, he wasn't seeing me at all.

Who would have thought I'd get something like that? Who ever thinks they'll get something? Who ever thinks they'll get what they get? Who gets what they think they'll get?

When dad was dying, the house became a depot. Trucks pulled up. Men — young men, muscled, alive — dropped off tanks of oxygen. Delivery vans pulled up with shipments of adult diapers. Little white delivery cars brought morphine. Nurses arrived in hatchbacks, leaving later that day.

This place smells. If you publish my memoirs (*Memoirs of a Recreation Director In Hell*, © 1992, the Recreation Director), I could find my true calling of being a writer. Every Wednesday the County Daycare sends over some children to brighten up the old peoples' day. Sam Woolley likes to get one of the children on his lap and whisper things in the child's ear. I know he is saying swear words. I went by and heard him say penis one time. The children are little monsters.

You refuse to acknowledge what you have seen by giving it the dignity of words. Or else you despair in what you've seen, in your inability to give it words. Either.

Once again, God had spared the widow.

"I don't like Christmas because Jesus died."
    "He didn't die at Christmas, stupid. He was born."
    " "

    "And anyway, if he didn't die, we wouldn't be able to go to heaven."
    "Oh."
    "We'd all have to go to hell."
    "Since Mindy doesn't believe, she has to go to hell, right, Sammy?"
    "I don't know."
    "Well she does."
    " "

8

"How many rubies do you have in the bank?"
"I don't know. Not many."
"You need a big ruby, Sammy."
"I know."

Everyone wants to be alone up to a certain point. After that point, no one wants to be alone. Could it be maybe, like, being alone gets like a habit? Like smoking? My dad smoked for thirty years. Then, one day, he quit. Ah, well. The years are like waterlogs. I'm sleeping.

Out of her office she comes. People were going in left, right and centre, I'm telling you, so I don't know what I was thinking. What was I thinking? People were really going in there like mad. Lots of people. And coming out again. These sorts of events should lead one to certain conclusions, wouldn't you think? Shouldn't they? Yes. They should.

The legs hang down over the edge of the bed. We couldn't afford to get the faucet centred properly on the wall. There was some kind of bylaw. We kept moving it around.
"We wouldn't have to worry about it," I started to say.
"Eventually, you have to worry about everything," she said.

Simple, yet strikingly lovely.

The bullet enters from the rear. Passes out the front. Tearing. Flesh cupping. Dripping. The black hair. The dust. There is no way of seeing. The bullet's origin. There is still breathing. Soon it will come clear. Things come into focus. Soon.

When I got down to the beach there was nothing to see. She told me about it later. Much later. I followed her down one afternoon, without her knowing I was there. The thing she wore fluttered. Like wind. If you stayed far enough back it was beautiful. If you stayed on the rocks, you could see the whole thing. Without the smell. The pebbles could have been sand.

It isn't as if she's asking to be who she is anymore. Who she is is no longer who she is.

It isn't as if she's asking to be someone else. She isn't asking to be someone else. She already always was somebody else. She already always was somebody else altogether than who she was. If people thought she was somebody who she wasn't, then people were wrong.

If people thought she was somebody who she wasn't, then they are assholes. She isn't the one who is the fucking asshole.

If anyone ever thought they ever knew who she was, that was exactly who she wasn't.

She was always somebody else altogether than who she was.

Who she is is long gone. Who she is never existed. If there was a who who she was, if there ever was such a who, if this who who she was, who everybody says she was, if this who who everybody says she was ever existed, this is a who who is long gone. This is a who who is so long gone it is as if this who never existed. Whoever it is who people think she is never existed.

Okay. Okay. Maybe she is exaggerating. Maybe who she is did exist. Maybe her saying who she is never existed is an exaggeration. Maybe. Maybe. Maybe this person who everybody thinks she is was who she is. Granted. Okay. Granted.

John advised his son: run across that field. As fast as you can. As fast as you can. When you can't run as fast as you can anymore, stop. Quick. Turn around and catch yourself coming back. It'll make you laugh. John laughed.

The first time we went down there, we all got burnt. We spent most of the holiday lying in bed, putting Noxema on our skin, and Grandma ran around looking nervous, saying, "Why did you do it?" or "I told you not to do it," or "You're getting grease all over the sheets."

After that, in later years, when we visited Grandma, we'd go out in the sun for a half hour only. And we'd turn ourselves regularly, like roasts.

Her name should be Breathed-Her-Own-Breath. If she had any say in the matter, her name would be Breathed-Her-Own-Breath. Breathed-Her-Own-Fucking-Breath. Although you'd never know it. You'd never know she had ever breathed her own fucking breath. You'd think everyone else had breathed her breath.

No matter how good of a tan you get, there's always someone around with a better one. One year, me and Tutti went to Greece. I thought, *I'm gonna get the best fuckin' tan ever.* And it happened. I came back home and nobody had a better tan. I went and visited everybody I knew and I thought, *There, you fuckers, top that.*

Five-thirty p.m. was a terrifying time. People left at 5:30 p.m. It was the end of everything.

Sammy was six. I wanted to go with him everywhere. He still held my hand when we went places.

When they were gone, it got quiet. There was a breeze. I could hear planes. I was glad to be where I was. You could always hear the cars out on the highway. You could hear the voices. Kids talking, but you couldn't hear what they were saying. I was happy.

I picked up the dog he took to bed every night and put it on the bed beside him. I hurried to my bed and lay on my back in the dark wishing something terrible. Something involving Crystal. Tutti was downstairs in the kitchen. Opening drawers. Cupboards. Removing spoons. Bowls.

I would go up after the kids were bathed and bedded, teeth brushed, faces shining, and kiss and hug them goodnight. I liked this little ritual more than anything. Everything else made me tired. I was tired at work. I was tired at home. I was tired going from work to home.

"How many feelings do we have?"

"Fifty."

"Look at those horses. Look at those cows." I honked the horn.
   "Don't honk the horn," she said.

Ask Patty what she means by feel good? Does she mean like when
I get all my Recreation profiles filed and still have time for a
smoke and watch Dr. Lance get a hard-on from touching all the
grannies? Or does she mean when I get to see the new nurse give
Enid J. Crackel a needle and she can't find a vein?

p.s. today is still Monday.

I had the weirdest dream about you. You phoned and you were
talking nonsense. There was a lot of noise going on in the room.
The phone cord was all tangled up. It was tangled like the phone
cord in my kitchen. But it wasn't my kitchen. It was like a camp
rec room. With a wooden counter at one end. And a loft. And
everything made out of cheap wood. Like panelling. There was a
doorway next to the phone leading to a hall. Just like at my house.
Only it wasn't my house. And I was standing in the hall trying to
hear what you were saying. It was utter nonsense. It was English.
It was a sort of chant. I could almost recognize words. I had in
my heart some understanding that it was sad. A desperate chant.
I think you might have called twice and the same chant thing
happened. Then we were no longer on the phone. I can't remember what happened after that. But after a time I tried to call you.
I had to use some strange system to decode your phone number
from something on the counter. It was like fast food containers.
A pizza box or something maybe. With some kind of prize you
could win if you decoded the message. Only it was your phone
number I was trying to figure out. I figured it all out and then
I was trying to get the last two digits when a dog came into the
rec room. It was on a leash. Something flew up over me and hit
the plywood across the loft above my head. A man in goggles
was there saying something to me about what had flown over
my head. Some silly joke-like comment about being careful. He

had the dog's leash. Then I decoded the last two digits. But I was almost sure I didn't get them right. But I must have because you picked up the phone and started chanting immediately, without saying hello or anything. But it was just a short chant this time. And I still couldn't understand you. Except it sounded sad. Like you were trapped in something. But at the end I heard exactly what you said and it was: "I have no life, just Maria, and you." I woke up. I went to check my email. Then I checked my voice mail. Your message was there.

"The drugged sound of her voice is a trap," said the librarian beside me. The librarian makes me happy. His quiet voice tells me cool ideas he has for making his library better. He wants a sign that says CLOSED in red neon.

Sometime around midnight I had a nightmare. I don't remember it at all, except that at the end I tried to scream and nothing came out. This was the same as my last nightmare a few nights ago when the lineup of men each received a note saying what disease they had and the last note had the most horrible disease and I was suddenly in the line of men and there was only me left and the last note with the most horrible disease was for me.

At work, I am going to be writing some documents for the new strategic plan.

I don't like Jesus because of Jed. The legs hang down over the edge of the world.

They say what he wrote was terrible. It didn't meet corporate standards. I want to see what he wrote. We hear a summary of who he was. They tell us he was small. He had no ability. I want to see what they saw before they reduced him to this small man unable to meet expectations. Where was he looking that he wasn't looking to meet their expectations?

I can't stay here. I know it. I'll stay here as long as I can. I won't even know when I'm no longer here. Then, suddenly, I'll be here again, and I'll realize I wasn't here all that time when I thought I was.

I have an idea to make the theme: "To really live, you have to really give." I'm not sure how it will play out in the first piece I write. It may be too overt to give to the library, but I'll write it blatant at first, and then tone it down, so the sound of it resonates in the piece in a way that won't scare the sons of bitches who always want to try to stop me. I'm excited to write this.

What if he was giving them one last chance? What if he was giving himself his own last chance? What if he determined to be really honest? To really honestly put himself in what he wrote for them? If he put himself in, he wouldn't be putting them in and if he wasn't putting them in, of course, he wouldn't be meeting their expectations, because they are always their own expectations. What if he put himself out so far beyond expectation that only the next word, not yet written, not yet imagined, could capture what was about to arrive?

...asked if I could really get high on life and I told her yes and she said I should tell her about it sometime. I never did. But I was thinking yesterday that the shivering might be a kind of withdrawal from the high I get just living these days. I get very high for very long periods of time and when I come down and feel calm...

...note under the covers so Tutti would find it when she got in bed. I figured I'd still be in Oshawa at that point.

Sammy and I got home at about 10 p.m. Tutti was still up, watching TV with Shortboy. The note was still there. She hadn't seen it. I took it and hid it so she wouldn't read it.

When the kids were asleep and Tutti came to bed, I told her I wanted to talk to her. She said, "Oh, no, not again," in that half-joke, half-serious way she has. I told her...well, I struggled a bit at first to say what I was trying to say. I told her I knew she didn't really like me touching her and that it made me lonely. I told her I thought she was afraid of me and she said she wasn't, but I said I thought she was. I told her I wanted her to be happy and that I would like to be the one who she was happy to see, but it didn't have to be me. I said if she wanted me to go out of her bed, I would and I would wait and hope she invited me back. She said she had nothing she could say right now. I said that was okay, she didn't have to say anything, but I wanted her to know I was lonely and I needed to be touched. I said I would turn off the light now and I did and we lay, each alone, for a moment. Then I rolled over toward her and said something and she said she just wanted to cry and I told her not to be stupid, she should cry on me. She finally turned and held me. And she cried a little more and really held me. We lay and held each other and we talked a bit more. I said how much I loved her and that I wanted her back and how beautiful I thought she was. I held her face between my hands and said…

I'm painting trim. Wearing my boxers. No shirt. Bare feet. Nike baseball cap. All the colour from the cap faded from blue to tie-dye purple. Tutti is out running. Sammy does homework. A magazine spread about the universe for his Languages course. I'm on a painting break, watching Shortboy play Donkey Kong.

Mavern Clark's husband dies of a massive brain hemorrhage while doing some plumbing. The psychologists here, Dr. Lamont and Dr. Svichtersternmann, think they can help these people but they cannot. There is no way to help them. I sometimes wish they would all die and make some room in this place for some nice old people whom I could take to the park. These people never bathe. I sent out a questionnaire asking them:

WHERE WOULD YOU LIKE TO GO:
1. interesting industrial plants
2. parks and scenic spots
3. or visit the state legislature

Lavyrle said let's just stay in the rec room. Maybe this gives you an idea of what I am dealing with here.

From the early '50s, Bill & I were the closest of friends. The hours we spent in my basement pad at Lumley & Heath — fireplace blazing, listening to the "Jupiter Symphony" by Mozart — harmonic, melodic — the depth of its simplicity — there were times when it was a challenge to our emotional state if we dare even listen to it. A highlight that stands out is when we went to Massey Hall for Glenn Gould's solo recital of the Goldberg Variations by Bach.

The father was quiet, sitting on the brown, straight-backed chair, among the other guests. In front of his eyes, his daughter was performing, her voice rising up, up past the steeples and tenements, the tall office towers, up past the clouds, joining the cosmic mathematics of God.

Behind the father, outside the window, God had spread his white coat over the land and was wandering alone into the fields where high school students brought girls on summer nights. God was scratching his beard, contemplating suicide. Garbage floated by in the river.

Tutti takes all of Sammy's pictures off the wall and puts them in the middle of the floor under where the light hangs down. This is 10:30 at night. Tutti taps her foot. "I'm throwing them out."

"Don't throw them out."

Tutti looks at me. Shakes her head. "You're just sad," she says.

The many hours we rehearsed & performed as a quartet at the House of Hambourg (Bill on tenor & piano) — then at Stratford's music festival with Norm Symonds' octet opposite Dave Brubeck's quartet. He was also in the band for a 1969 concert in Detroit with Duke Ellington. When I was involved in a controversial issue at Humber College, it was Bill & Gord Delamont who without hesitation gave me their support. But most of all, in those early years, Bill was my true friend. In those "20 something" years we probed the meaning of where, what, how, why, when & why not!

I lean over and pick up all the pictures, roll them up in a big bundle, all the pictures Sammy ever made since before he was two, since he ever even started making pictures. I roll them all up. These are all of Sammy's pictures since he was a little boy. All of them. "Go to bed," I tell Tutti.

When Kathy & I got married in 1959, there was no question, Bill was my best man. Then as all things go, new relationships materialize, you buy a house, have kids, jobs change, etc. Social contacts change and we lose touch.

I take the bundle of pictures down to the basement. I go over to the laundry cupboard. I pull out all the boxes of laundry detergent Tutti got on a deal. There are dozens of boxes of laundry detergent back there. I stuff the bundle of pictures into the back of the cupboard and push all the laundry detergent back in. Then I stand beside the washing machine, crying.

At the service on Nov. 26, the highlight for me was the saxophone quartet playing "There'll Never Be Another You" — a tune that Bill & I played so many times together. And finally the applause at the end that said, "We were all so fortunate to have known Bill Sparling."
    My heart wept with joy.
    All my love, Ron Collier.

Fuck you, Ron Collier.

Sam Woolley told Enid Crackel that the only way to experience a heightened sense of awareness within today's tragic milieu is to take mind-expanding drugs. Enid told Sam to kiss her ass. I have been reading about the tragic need to help old people develop their powers of sensitivity and awareness. I told Enid she must contemplate truth and justice, life and death, God and man and freedom and responsibility if she wants to broaden the dimensions of her awareness. She told me to go get laid. Lavyrle then came in smoking a cigarette which got stuck to her lip and she couldn't get it off because she couldn't let go of her walker, so it burned her lip and she screamed. Everybody just stood watching her get her lip burned and I thought, *it serves her right*, but I ran over and pulled the butt out of her mouth. I don't know how I am expected to enrich the lives of these idiots. I no longer know what my mission statement should be. I have read all the literature in the field. I am at a loss. This place smells. You have to get me out of here. I don't know how I am expected to deal with these people.

He went into a room and closed the door behind him. The room was round with white walls and a white ceiling and white tiles on the floor. It was a bright room with no windows. Just bright light coming from someplace he couldn't see. The only object in the room was a chair. But this seemed like enough. He entered the room. Went to the chair. Sat. He put his hands in his lap. He looked inside himself. He thought this should be enough. And for a while it was. But at a certain point, thinking it should be enough made it not enough and he felt a desire to get up and leave the room and find something to do in the world he'd left before he entered the room. There was plenty to do in that world. There were many responsibilities. Many reasons to be. He felt this stirring inside him to move. But he didn't get up. He felt heavy. Incapable of moving. But he knew, deep inside himself, that he wanted to stay in the room. So he stayed.

He sat a long time. Nothing happened. The room stayed empty. Sometimes he remembered the world outside. He remembered a woman he had known and his being grew heavy and his soul felt crushed. At other times, he felt nothing. Just the room around him and the chair beneath him and not even those things seemed really to be there and his mind drifted over moments and sometimes these moments were things he could be doing and sometimes his mind drifted over the woman he'd remembered. But these things his mind wandered over laid no claim and his mind moved on and he sat alone in the room.

Soon the heaviness returned. But now it seemed to come out of his soul. And it crushed his will to move. And it crushed his will to do the things he'd done in the world before he entered the room or to meet with the woman he remembered or the children he recalled from that world. He thought now if he left the room he would carry this heaviness with him wherever he went and he would deposit it on all the world and colour it heavy and then he would have to endure this heaviness, not just inside himself in his soul, but also in everything he confronted in the world, including the woman and the children he remembered. By now he had almost completely forgotten that he stayed in the room only because he wanted to. But it was still true. He still stayed in the room for no reason other than his desire to stay there, and he thought he heard someone pounding on the door and he thought it must be the woman and he covered his head to block out the pounding and he fell to the floor and he curled up in a ball and held himself and rocked and he felt like the density of the entire universe had contracted into one little spot inside him and he wanted it to stop hurting him like this.

When he opened his eyes he saw that the woman was sitting on the floor with her back to the wall. Her legs were splayed out in front of her and her hair was matted and hanging over her face and her face was blotchy and spotted from crying and the children sat on either side of her, close, under her arms, and they looked scared, eyes wide and faces empty. The man realized that this woman and these children had been in the room with him all along and he picked himself up and he went to the woman and children and pushed the woman's hair away from her face and he touched her wet cheeks and she sobbed a little and then her shoulders shook and she cried so hard she looked like she would break and he watched her cry and he leaned toward her.

You think Dad dying is a hard thing? Fuck it. Imagine believing someone was so important. Is that what you want from the people who love you? Then fuck off. Just fuck off.

I sent Wilma e-mails and she e-mailed back. She was living in California at that time. She and her husband, Carl. One of her sons, Carl Jr., was also in California. Carl Jr. had just recently married. He and his bride had done a six-month tour of the world.

They travelled to places like Tibet. When they got back, Carl Jr.'s wife, Wanda, found a job in her field, which is social work, and Carl Jr. tried to figure out what to do with his life. Before he'd met Wanda, Carl Jr. had been a house painter. But house painting was hurting his back.

When my sister called on the phone and Gretchen put the phone up to Dad's ear, and my sister said whatever it was she said to Dad, how did Gretchen know when to pull the phone away from Dad's ear and get back on the line herself?

Really what it was was a sort of freedom from myself. Does that seem better? I measured everything in terms of myself. What I was experiencing now felt like nothing so much as an escape. I would die. After Dad died, I knew. I could die at any moment. Whatever was happening now, in a minute I might be dead. It felt good. I knew that when I died, no matter what anybody said, my family, my sons, my wife, everyone would feel a kind of a relief. A sort of freedom.

Getting buried, getting burnt, I wasn't particular about either option. I'd think about my end, and think about whether I would get burnt or buried, and it didn't seem to make a whole lot of difference. But maybe getting burnt would be better.

I heard about these people in stories Wilma sent me in her e-mails. Sometimes I sent stories back. Stories about the kids. But the kids were going insane at that time. One night the power went off at 2 a.m. and Shortboy woke up screaming in his crib and tried to rip off all his clothes. He had just turned two. We went into his room and found him standing naked in his crib, crying. I had a flashlight. I went to Shortboy and got him out of his crib. He tried to hit me. But he was only two. It didn't hurt much. I took him down to the kitchen. Walked around in circles. Told stories until he stopped crying. Then I took him up to bed with Tutti and me and pretty soon he was asleep.

But I couldn't sleep. I lay awake wondering what was happening here. Afraid of what was happening. I started asking God for help. It was the same as always. The God I knew was not a god who listened to prayers.

I kept waiting for the power to come on. It was growing cold. The heater couldn't come on without the power to run the blower. I couldn't pull the covers up over me because I was afraid of disturbing Shortboy.

The next night, Shortboy did the same thing. He woke up crying, trying to get his clothes off. This time I took his clothes off for him. After that he wanted some milk. So I got him some milk. Then I brought him into bed with me and Tutti.

I woke up at 4:30 a.m. and Shortboy was sleeping. I put a diaper on him. Then I went back to sleep, secure in the knowledge that he would not wet our bed.

Mostly what I heard about in Wilma's e-mails was stories about her parents. My grandparents. Wilma sent these stories whenever she had time, but apparently she didn't have much time. I think she was so busy staying in touch with everyone. Actually, I don't know what she was busy doing. She played golf. She did volunteer work for some charities. I know how those charities can be. When she was in town, I saw her. It was never for more than a few hours. And then the kids were usually around, so we didn't have time to talk. Two days after Dad died, Wilma came to town and I went to see her for a few hours without the kids. She showed me some pictures. I have photocopies of some of those pictures.

I wanted to try to develop some characters, so people would come back to my story hoping to hear about these wonderful characters I'd created. They'd read for a while, then look up and think, *this guy makes good characters.*

We sat at the dining room table. All of us. On the table were stacks of photographs and photograph albums. The idea was to get pictures together for the memorial service. Wilma showed us a picture of Dad when he was two. Outside it was raining. It was already December. But the rain would not turn to snow. The phone kept ringing and one or the other of the girls would go out to the kitchen to answer it.

Hold it, where the hell are you going? Turn there.
    I was just driving in a straight line.

Come on, he said, and he pulled on his hat and walked out the door and I followed him.
    Where are we going? I asked. He was walking fast. Faster than I'd thought anyone could walk without running. I kept bursting into short running spurts to try to catch up.
    Where the hell are we going?
    To the car.
    The car?
    We kept going out across the field. I could see for miles. But I couldn't see any car.
    There's no car.
    It's over the top of the rise.
    There's no rise.
    He stopped suddenly and I nearly bumped into the back of him.
    Look, he said, you'll never get anywhere walking. These fields go on for hundreds of miles. If you want to get anywhere, we'll have to drive. Now just trust me for once.
    Why?
    Ha ha.
    He started walking again. I turned back to look at the cabin and it was gone. Hey, I said, but I didn't say anything else. Before too long, I could see something shiny on the horizon, and pretty soon that something shiny became a car.
    We drove for what might have been hours, or maybe days. Although it couldn't have been days, because it never got dark. There was an AM radio in the car, but it only got one country and western station. Still, it somehow seemed appropriate. I hadn't listened to country and western music since I worked for the Parks Department while I was at University. God, the places you wind up on this trip.

I know, he said.
Did I say that out loud?
You did.

That was how she put it. "If there was a good way for it to happen," she said, "this was it. He died peacefully. In his bed. At home. Before he died we had time to say everything we had to say to each other."

"Scouting out hiding places?" I ask. None of us knows what I am talking about. They laugh and nod. "Preferably someplace with no windows," I add, still not knowing. The weeds in ditches were gone long before I checked. Their existence a legend.

We enter the reception area. Fall silent. I follow two inclinations into another space. No one speaks. When we get to the offices, they go into one together, talking quietly as I move away.

A writer in a bookstore will talk to you in his actual voice.

I thought, as I sat in the cafeteria reading Katherine Paterson's revised *Who Am I?*, that there was no way I could tell people what I knew. But then I decided I'd go for it anyway. So far it's just this, and it's the same thing again and again. Imagine that evil is nothing more than making plans, setting goals, going for it. Imagine that my decision to try to tell you what I know is itself evil. Imagine that evil saturates every part of getting out of bed each morning and taking steps to get ready for work.

As per our discussion at the December 14 meeting, I wish to confirm that staff would be interested in name tags for their babies. A rough estimate for a one-year supply would be as follows: [something follows]. Please keep me informed.

Last minute details taking place all day. Met with Andy, Rick and Billie. Heard the tinkling of the bells. Will resume calls once training is done. Committed to the latest morph. The spots will return. On Wednesday, Mother died. Alice to be debriefed due to absence last week. Hum hum hum. Revisions complete. First colour draft complete. Obtained approval and proceeded. Worked on something all day. Slept. Woke up. Something in me did not wake. Other parts woke. Slipped on canvas shoes. Left. They might take that back and see if anyone wants some local conversation. Transmissions to start this week. Should feel less important. We will be aware.

It was 5:30 p.m. and the sun had gone down and I was driving home. Whenever I tried to put my gloves on, the Band-Aid rolled up and pulled the hair on the back of my hand, so I stopped trying to put my gloves on. I put my bare hands on the steering wheel and drove. Nothing big was happening. Everything that was happening was small. The biggest thing I could think of to say was that everything was small and that nothing was very big anymore. There was nothing of any consequence or bigness anymore.

It was a small packet of flesh. It was square. We'd named it Barbara. I held it in my arms. It had no legs.

I was my son. I knew what it felt like to be my son. I was talking to one of my son's friends. I said, "We need the goggles." We had both heard about the goggles.

Kids are very interested. They are helping each other. Most of them have had their troubles.

Hi. I'm Matthew, son of Roxanne, the Wal-Mart cashier. Roxanne was my mom. She's dead now. My dad was the guy who did the barbecuing. Mom used to bring things home. It was fall. The river nearly flooded. Mom started putting sugar on her toast.

He'd sit on his bike and I would stand in front of him and read him some poems. He would sit for a moment, looking at the sky, as though thinking. Then he would get one of his feet up onto one of the pedals, and with his other foot he would push off and he would ride out my driveway and along the road. I would stand still in the driveway with my poems in my hand.

I went to the Goodwill store. At the back, they had used books. They'd sell any used crap. They sold it to raise money for the poor. The people working in the store were poor. When you went to the cash to pay for something, it was a member of the poor who served you. That's why you could feel good about buying that crap.

The man in ankle-length socks appeared many weeks later, when the weather had cooled off and the old man and the boy felt comfortable returning to the city.

Indeed, it is you, Bill. There was a dog at the end of the street. Like a hotdog. In lieu of falling, I decided to lunge. Dog; Bill; translucent girl at Bill's side.

Could we stop them? Why did we do this? Maybe this is that. Maybe the only way in is the way they do that where the five of them are only another excuse for something no one can put their fingers on.

Parts of me are disappearing. My husband is a skeleton. Red light means stop. My boots make me taller. People are made of triangles. Their hair doesn't move. The fingers are wafers. His small beard is located on the corner of his chin. Give us mercy, Susan. What was she talking about? What was the rule for choosing fonts?

You'll discover that some wear sunglasses. The committee met. In the room with flies, the light hurt. Tom the Alcohol Inventor spoke. Outside, on the grass, dogs murmured. "I'm not afraid, Len." Light blazed. Inside backup tunnel number four, men in yellow helmets trembled. Roger held the note fourteen inches from the sky.

The committee met annually in the room with Tom the Alcohol Inventor. The light hurt the committee. Everyone's eyes outside on the lawn. Dogs spoke among themselves. I'm not afraid, Len said. Light blazed inside the city's men. Yellow helmets trembled. Roger held the note.

You'll discover some wear sunglasses. You'll discover committees. You'll meet. In the room with flies, the light will hurt your eyes. You'll stumble upon Tom the Alcohol Inventor. Outside, on the grass, you'll hear dogs. You'll hear them say they are not afraid. You'll see light. You'll meet men in yellow helmets. You'll tremble. You'll hold notes. You'll see the sky.

One year he got a big wooden cottage with a screened-in front room. I think everyone was there that year. Grandma and Grandpa Sparling. Aunt Wilma. Uncle Carl. Our cousins. Shannon, Carl Jr. and Ronnie.

When Sammy was three, he tried to pick up a bee he saw on the beach. It stung him on the thumb. We didn't know what happened. He was screaming. Looking at his hand. Then we saw the bee on the sand and Sammy's thumb swelling up. Now Sammy doesn't like to go into the park behind our house because there are so many bees back there.

Which makes evil absolutely sociopathic. Completely outside the bounds of the social. Without reference to the social. There are, then, no deliberately evil people. Evil is a pathology whose very soul is delimited in its absolute obliviousness to deliberation.

The tall woman in the border shack jumped. Turned to face the others. The green light coming in. Through the windows. The others like statues. Waiting for the light.

My sister was over. Doing dishes. Putting them away in the wrong places. My husband came in. "We're out of propane." He had the propane tank. "These things are pretty heavy. Even empty." He smirked at my sister. He went out. "What an asshole." Later, when my sister had gone home to her husband and babies, and my husband was in bed, dreaming whatever dreams he dreams, I took all the dishes out, even the ones my sister hadn't put there. I put them on the counter. I went out into the night.

"Same thing."
    "Is not."
    "No? Then why do you look like one?"
    "I don't."
    "Do too."
    "Do not."
    "Yes you do. Look at yourself."
    I looked at myself.

"Are you still angry?"
    "No."
    "Yes you are."
    "No I'm not."
    "Are too."
    "Are not."
    "Are."
    "Not."

"It could be many things."
    "No it couldn't."
    "Yes it could."
    "Could not."
    "Could so."

Jagged and torn. That was the structure. And right back at the beginning again. Always. But don't tell anyone. And now things seem to be coming together. The torn apart thing. So far that's how I've known. I'm the guy who can make the moments jump out and matter.

I think my son is getting more and more scared. He sits in front of the TV like everything is far ahead of him and he can't get there and he isn't even trying anymore.

Some people seem to have less dimensions. They are harmless. Maybe that's exactly the point. It's like they never had anything taken away. And then they willingly relinquished something. I think it has a lot to do with something.

You have to give up everything. Eventually. You have to say, *I'm not a lesbian. I'm not a teacher. I'm not Gordon.*

I pick the night before. I grab fast. First a shirt. Then some pants. I wear one pair of underwear all week. I get the socks last. I put them in a pile and set them on the floor downstairs.

All narrators have good skin. They are skinny with slightly unkempt hair. They have something beautiful inside them and it can never get out.

I never realized how far apart you have to be to be together.

I know I hope if I am ever in a coma I will know if something someone is saying is something they really want to say or if it's something they are saying because they think they have to say it. I certainly hope that by the time I wind up in a coma, I'm in a position to know certain things. Jesus, you'd think you would have earned it by then. Especially if the coma was from dying of cancer.

When we were kids, me and my sister, we wanted Dad to quit smoking. We were afraid it was going to kill him.

I went into Enid Crackel's room yesterday at nap time. Enid was sitting up in bed saying a poem to herself and crying. I have never seen Enid Crackel cry before. I asked her if I could do anything to help. She said yes, I could go fuck myself. I went to the staff lounge and recited my mantra. Then Dr. LaRoque came in with the new nurse, laughing and giggling together. The whole thing makes me sick.

You asked him all the wrong questions.

I didn't ask him any questions. I made all that stuff up.

Exactly. Jesus. You know you're in trouble when you make up interviews with your dad after he's dead and even then you can't get the questions right.

Do you support the teachers?
    No. But I don't support the Board of Education either. I support any reasonable measures used to obtain reasonable ends.
    They won't reason.
    Have you given up reasoning with them?
    Yes.
    That's what I don't support. Get on with your day. At the end of that day, use reasonable means to work toward what you feel you need in order to do a better job. Let other people know what you feel you need. Talk about it. Nothing happens overnight.

The boys are playing. Nintendo. I'm sitting on the deck. In a towel. I've been in the lake. It's cold. It's 8 in the morning. Tutti still in bed. It isn't raining. It will. I've got coffee. A spider comes out of a crack in the siding.

Write out the figuring. Even if you never finally figure it. Even if you never get to the end of the figuring.

The man who couldn't sleep.
    The man who couldn't sleep at 2 a.m.
    The man who couldn't sleep on Sundays.
    The man who couldn't sleep after eating chicken.
    The man who couldn't sleep in a bed.
    The man who couldn't sleep at the cottage.
    The man who couldn't sleep on the beach.
    The man who couldn't sleep in the lake.
    The man who couldn't sleep in Fresno.
    The man who couldn't sleep near a toaster.
    The man who couldn't sleep in his underwear.
    The man who couldn't sleep underwater.
    The man who died.
    The man who never died.

Robert Schumann tried to stretch his fingers to play better piano. Just the fact that he did this shows us something. Crippling his fingers. A huge gamble. A desire. Find a good reason to die. As soon as possible.

She put things on the bed. Folded things. Stacks of clean under-wear. They smelled from being outside. She folded the underwear. Lay it on spaces on the bed. She dumped stacks of ironing on the bed. Stood beside the bed, ironing. Singing. She came into the room. Closed the window. Threw open the curtains. Ironed.

One day Tutti came into the bedroom and told me to act like a living entity. "Put on some underwear," she told me. "Put on some socks. And a shirt. And some pants."

It was spring. We were going for a walk. To the mall. To get buttons. Tutti knew a store at the mall that had buttons.

I had to go on peoples' lawns to keep from getting a soaker. Every time there was less water on the sidewalk and I got back beside Tutti, Tutti licked her hand and reached over and tried to make some of the pieces of my hair that were sticking up on my head go down. I sensed this was some kind of turning point. I thought, *Tutti is going to ask me to go walking places with her all the time now.*

I don't know where it came from, but what I did was, I looked at the farm fields and I noticed how nicely one house sat in front of a hill. That didn't seem to help. I thought, *Well, I didn't put that house there.* Tammy came by to throw her Popsicle stick out. She smiled. Her lips looked swollen. I wanted to kiss them. But she was only nine.

He knew what privacy meant. There was nothing but surface. Illusion. A preoccupation with surface was the gift. From God. *Thank you, God*, he thought. He thought he saw the depths. But as soon as the surface pulled away, as soon as he turned his face, hid his face, the depths evaporated. He was like a flag. In wind. Depth was the yawning silence. Beneath the noise of silence. A silence.

It isn't the moment I'm living. It's that moment just ahead. Just in front. It's when I look away I'm lost. It's that moment I'm about to fall into. The rain not yet come. Me sitting. On the deck. Waiting.

Today was Charade Day. Sam Woolley couldn't figure out what Enid Crackel was trying to be. Enid kept pulling on her ear. Sam started kicking her. I can't stand this. Enid Crackel cackles like a witch. Lavyrle falls off her walker. Sam Woolley cries all the time. Help me, you prick. One day your scrawny little ass will be in here with the rest of them and then you will see just who the Recreation Director is.

I have enemies. In the world. Deliberation for example. Planning. Preparation. That recognition of what you have. A situation.

I don't look in the mirror anymore. Except once in the morning. And sometimes once in the afternoon, to make sure nothing is hanging out of my nose.

I've been glancing at things. All the talk about something deeper — something below the surface, something underneath what you are seeing — it's a kind of horror, isn't it? If you let them, people will tell you their theories on stuff.

We got long hotdogs. Sat on a bench. In a park. I watched the mustard. I tried to keep the mustard off my lips. The air was hot. You could smell the ducks. Kids threw bread crumbs. I ate my hotdog. Slowly. Always watching the mustard. After the last bite, I sat for a while. I remembered other hotdogs I had eaten.

Is it one of the kids' birthdays? What does the house look like? What are they eating? I need a good first sentence. Names of everyone.

There are two doors into every mall. Like an airlock. He holds the first door. She holds the second. They pass the place with the cinnamon buns. She is skinny. He looks at her bum. Senior citizens power walk. Snow falls outside. All day the light feels like dusk.

"It feels like some kind of mistake," he says.

"I think it is a mistake," she says. "A misjudgement."

One time, I was taking the tinsel off the Christmas tree. One strand at a time. The sun was sneaking through the cracks in the blinds. I kept taking tinsel off the tree. I was in the living room. Sun splashing on the carpet. I was slipping tinsel out between the dried up needles of the Christmas tree.

For a moment I was in a movie, fingertips on the table, the whole world watching. And then I realized what was happening and what time it was.

Tutti's sister Marble doesn't say a word when we outline the plot. Marble is in a bad mood. She doesn't have a job. Tutti's brother called from P.E.I. "You are the dregs of life, Marble," he said. Marble stays home. Bakes all day.

"You look like Heat Miser, Marble," I say.

Tutti and I laugh our heads off.

Marble laughs, too. "You're a jerk," she says. "Who the hell is Heat Miser?"

Me and Tutti laugh.

"Only Tutti would know instantly who Heat Miser is. You two make me sick." Marble looks sick.

It was Matty, though, who I was talking to, if you get what I am saying. It was Matty who I'd been saying things to all along. Whenever I imagined saying things, it was Matty I imagined saying them to.

Cool as a cucumber. That's how those walls were. Creamy, like salad dressing. Same as with Matty. But with Matty, you've got her lumpy body to think of.

It was the way the words were. Some arrangement in the words. There was something in the way the words came along, one after the other. It didn't seem like there was any way you were ever going to be able to stop them.

You get the idea that maybe Matty was kind of goofy.

He said it was big. A big empty field. We went out his front door. Crossed the road. He unzipped his pants.

I think we were both waiting for me to contradict him. When that silence fell, it wasn't just me thinking I should contradict him.

I'm thinking now of all that space in the gymnasium at school where you went sometimes and no one was there.

When I sit in her office, and I look out her window, what I'm looking for is something I can point out to Matty, because so far none of any of it is a thing I could point to.

I know what comes next. I know what comes after what comes next.

He gets the basketball right away.

None of this will make any sense.

When I'm crying, I know what comes next. I know what comes after the leaves have blown off the trees. I know what comes after the grass flattens in the wind. Everyone knows.

The sun will come out again. Eventually. But when?

What I'm trying to tell you is, I know what comes after the cows and the cream-coloured bands and the moment when Cal gets his fly unzipped. I know what comes next. I know.

The way she sat. Dabbing her eyes. Her eyes all red. Like she was crying. But it was the wind. They had to stop because of the wind.

Okay. You get what I'm saying. I'm in Matty's office. All I can think to say to Matty is: "Your skirt is going up." But it's the old couple I'm thinking of. The way they have to go slow in the wind. And then they have to stop. They actually have to stop. They have to come to a complete stop. For just a thing like the wind.

I've been touched. I've been touched all over. On every part of my body. That has to be taken into consideration. If you want to understand. Me telling things to Matty. How goofy Matty looks. But then, later, she doesn't seem so goofy.

She has cows all over her office. Stuffed cows. All the things I've said. All the things I've imagined saying. Take that and add the cows.

To him it feels like a game. Baseball. He's just made a spectacular catch. The runner crosses home plate. The umpire calls the runner safe. He looks at the ball. The ball is right there. Right there in his fucking glove.

I may forget. A thing like that. He would come into the bedroom. We had our PJs on. It was the cottage. We were in bunk beds. Dad rubbed our backs.

It's a relational thing. You enter variables into words. Words are brought into a play of contexts. Relations point at themselves. Toward each other. Directing someone's attention. The author of intention. My kid on the phone. "Look at this, Daddy." He holds something up. To the phone. "See." He knows all there is to know. I know nothing. Artifice. Relations. Space. Throwing relations into space. Throwing them out beyond. Same as God. Making all us people. Then leaving us here.

I wanted to search for and replace certain words which had occurred with great frequency in my life. I tried to think of all the words I had ever spoken in my life. I tried to see them as discrete bits of data. Data with codes attached. The words were no longer codes for something else. Rather, the codes were needed to get to the words. If you didn't have the codes, you couldn't get to the words. One of the words I wanted to replace was *sconce*.

He popped up the lid of the cockpit and stepped out onto what was left of the wing. The jet had made it most of the way through Wal-Mart. It had stopped just short of the cafeteria. He went up to a woman in a puce-coloured sweater whose Wal-Mart name badge said Marge. "Can you direct me to the section with the gas line antifreeze, Marge?"

To further circumambulate anent of arrival, the further your maunder of ipseity-gorans. Discrete moments of your self were still retrievable. At any rate, you reach a point. Turnancy requires a face of desolation (mesa of chipped and strewn rock): the only reckoning construable in the silence approaching death.

People feel pretty good when they laugh, so they like to laugh every chance they get. Laughing is about all you get these days. It is also supposed to be medicinally beneficial, which is a real bonus for those attempting to extend their time on this earth so they can squeeze in a few more laughs. You don't get a lot of the deep heartfelt sadness these days. Laughing is about the best you can actually hope for anymore.

The other day it was in the lunch room. It was the article where the old wife backed the car over her old husband killing him. It happened in the driveway. One of the guys here actually saw the dead guy lying under the car. It happened just down the street from here.

The nature article came about a week after an Indonesian researcher said he had redated a fossil fragment back one million years. This puts the origin of protohumans — the model upon which humans were later developed — at about two billion years ago this March. This predates the origins of the earth by approximately four months and is equivalent to the number of megabytes of hard disk space available on my son's computer. Bone fragments thought to date back to the Christmas of 4,213,133 BC were discovered in a geological formation known as the Chair of Ribena (near the town where the drink is produced).

Mom cried. God got in the car. Faced the front windshield. She would have seen trees. Beyond the trees, she might have seen the other townhouses. She wouldn't have seen beyond that. She may not have seen beyond the water in her eyes. She backed the little car into the road. Drove. Waved. Her face gone. The car gone. I went in the house. The book on the table. The red markings. It was sad. But there it was.

I was wearing my blue shirt. I was in my workspace. I was. Really.

It's so sad. I'm going to die. That makes me sad. So sad. Others will die. My dad already died. Grandpa is holding on by a thread. Not to mention accidents and natural disasters. The forest flying up beyond Grandpa's place. A sight he can't even behold. His eyes fucked for some years now. But I've seen that forest fly up beyond his place like God lost in a river. God happy to be lost. God lost to us. God lost to himself. God just lost. The river fills with rain. The river runs almost vertical with rain. (Not really. But it is quite a hill. Sammy and I climbed the sun-dappled fucker once. Nothing up there. We kept going. It seemed like we would keep going forever, but we decided not to. We came back.)

As long as you stay in the parking lot, you can remain parked. I tried to tell her this. She looked at me across the tiny space between the seats. "Again?" she said. I put the van in reverse and backed out of the parking spot. I thought this an achievement. I looked at her. She smiled. But she looked tired.

"Let's just get home," she said. "You can park the van in the driveway and just leave it parked."

We'd be in the house of course. And then there'd be tomorrow. I tried to tell her this, but only to the extent that you try to tell someone something without actually putting it into words. I'm not sure she understood.

They sit on a bench with their coffees. There are knives in a show-case across from them. One knife is a Swiss Army Knife.

"That thing's got nose hair clippers," he says.

"What?" She turns.

"That Swiss Army Knife." He points. She laughs. "I feel like I'm trapped," he says.

"I know."

They sit side by side.

"Listen to this poem." He pulls out a piece of paper from his pocket. Unfolds it. He reads the poem. It has nothing to do with anything. He realizes this as he reads. But it's too late to stop reading. The last line of the poem is one word: *Asshole*. He folds the paper back up.

I was reading a book. I went to the window. Looked out. The units across the street. Rain in the trees. I opened the window. Someone's car door slammed. I tried to see who it was. I went downstairs. Stood in the kitchen. The boys were asleep.

Angel had ten dollars on March 13. She showed me. She showed me her ten-dollar bill. She leaned close to me. I could smell things on her. I could see the space between her fingers.

"That guy just put his Cadillac on the front lawn," she called. She was upstairs. The mother was downstairs. In the kitchen.

"What," the mother called.

She ran over to the door. Put her head in the hall. "It's the man from the Cadillac, Mom. Don't let him in." She ran back over to the window. Looked down. The streetlights lighting up her face.

Both kinds of weather, warm and cold, can exist together, can make you aware of their presence simultaneously. The two, warm and cold, are unable to mix on certain days. Not like hot and cold water. Enjoy the faces and the walk and that young girl over there in the sweater.

The Christmas lights come on. In the tree outside. Sammy and Shortboy talk about a TV show they've been watching. Tutti is out in the car. Headlights on. She backs the car out. Drives out of sight. Dinner is in the oven.

My cousin was at the door. Waiting to get in. This was two years ago. It was snowing. I let her in.

The girls came at 8 in the morning. Every morning. I didn't usually see them. I was on my way to work by then. Twice that year, I had dinner with Dad. I began to wonder how long I could keep this up.

Behind the woman. Water lapping the shore. Water falling from the sky. I step out. In the distance there are things no one sees. Air hits me. Something falls. A long way off. The sound of gravel. The tires roll. I step forward into my footsteps.

I have dreams. In all my dreams, I am afraid.

It's the kind of wind that lifts things up, and all I can think of to say is, *Your skirt is going up, Matty.*

It was like the edge of something that nobody else had seen. Cathy hadn't seen it. She was giving routine instructions to the children who were sitting in a circle holding out their hands.

The heat was on. It was blowing. The air blows up across the inside of the windshield. The windshield seems a far way off. But I could feel it, the hot wind of heat on my forehead. Lifting my hair.

The twins were there. They were a moment on the beach I hadn't expected. Sand gritty on my skin. Wind. The twins' hair behind them. Their flesh leaking. Their diligent efforts to look different, one from the other. And Jennifer in her bikini, larger up top, but belonging so much more than either of the twins that the wind had no resonance within her.

I thought I could make it work. We talked about Tony. What he looked like before he died. Angel said he looked awful. We laughed. I ordered coffee. We had nothing to talk about. I asked about her children.

Tutti and I lay awake. For an hour. Talking. I couldn't get the whole thing sorted out. Finally I asked Tutti: "Do you support the postal workers?"

"I don't know, honey," she said. She moved closer to me. I didn't want her to touch me. She had the flu. I didn't want to get the flu.

It's not like there's nothing but cows. She has her husband. And kids. The cows make me think of something else, though. It's the cows, but when I go to think of them, it's something else. Like when I'm talking to Cal, but really I'm talking to Matty.

She's reaching for this or that on her desk, pulling open a drawer. Leaning.

It makes me think of something else, and sometimes I think maybe I could tell a person what that something else is. I'll look out the window and think there is something out there that matches the something I am thinking.

It isn't just cows.

The whole thing of the cream-coloured bands is that everybody in the room knows they are there. Everybody. Meaning: I'm not the only one who knows. But the colour that actually enters your head when you see the cream-coloured bands is the colour of something raw.

As Recreation Director, I am often called upon to write publicity for upcoming events. Please consider my manuscript (you have not received it yet, but will shortly). It is a story of a young nurse who has an affair with one of the residents at the old age home where she works. It is not autobiographical. At staff meetings, we discuss the need to reduce situations wherein patients lie in their feces. The important thing is not to panic. Sam Woolley came into the rec room crying yesterday. He took away the paddle Enid was using to play ping-pong with Lavyrle. Enid gets her grandson to bring her ping-pong balls. Sam says he doesn't belong in the home, that he is, in fact, only 49. I tell you all of this only to let you know that my life here is a living hell as I am responsible for monitoring order in the rec room. Stop wasting space on Enid Crackel as her life is almost over and I am in my prime and you could be publishing my memoirs on the ground floor, *Memoirs of A Recreation Director in Hell* (copyright 1992, the Recreation Director) in serial form.

People send me things. And they make me cry. Then I think of Uncle Albert in Mary Poppins. How happy it made him when people came to visit. And how he cried whenever people had to go away. Then I think about Dad dying of cancer. Then I vow to stop thinking.

We were in the same bed. She might have been crying. It doesn't matter. Either she was crying or she wasn't. If she wasn't, it's all the same. I'll never know. I don't even know why I want to know. It seems like we made some kind of pact to try to see into each other, but most of the time I don't even try.

Mom thought it was great that I could make her laugh. But it wasn't. It was the only way I could survive. I had to make her laugh or I was dead. I had no choice. No one does. Whenever you think you have a choice, you don't. You don't do anything by choice. Everything you do, you have to do. If you think you are doing something by choice, it just means you aren't doing anything.

The girl with the painted eyes. Dark hair like rags. Old acne. She let her arms fall to her sides. Like she was through with them. Forever. Her eyelids fell. Like torn rags. In wind. They're like wounds. She winked like a wound closing. Shreds of mascara kissed her eyes. Touching one wound to another. Something in that kiss would speak to him. And he would feel at ease. But she was gone. "I'll call you," she called. But she moved away like a gorged lioness not interested in another bite.

He worked on finding things his horse would notice. He lived on the ridge. We lived in the valley. I could see his smoke rising. "Go to bed," Mom said.

There was nothing I could do. I walked up the ridge. The clouds above. Like things we might have touched on a different day. In a different age. The earth lay in clumps beneath my feet. My shoes. The illusion of motion. The culmination of segregate positions. The liquid positionless swirl of time.

I had the child by the scruff of the neck.

There was a child on the swings. His mother was pushing him. The child was singing a song. He was little.

By means of purposefully misguided trajectory, the punks implicated error into their work. Each repetition braved the purely human. Barred God from entering with his pureness for the sake of pureness. For the beautiful meaninglessness of it. As meaningless as the moment the toad sits alive in the belly of the snake and waits. *We're food*, the punks seem to be saying. *We need to do some spitting when we sing.*

Ralph went down to the kitchen. Put a bowl on a tray. Poured cereal. Added milk. Got a glass. Filled it. Orange juice. Took the tray upstairs. Sat on the bed. He could see his father's face. The side of his father's face. "I'm having Cheerios," he said. His father was still in a coma.

Bertrand did nothing. Moved no part of his body. Blinked maybe. Once. Then opened his eyes to June. She felt his care. How careful he was. How being careful was his oeuvre.

He pushed the bike out the door. Stood under the sun. The thunk of the door shuddering in the warm air behind. Until a silence settled within the envelope of traffic noise coming over the houses from the highway below.

He put one foot on a pedal and pushed.

He had been inside since 9 o'clock. Most of the day slipped by. He rode to recapture. As much as to say, *These few minutes are accounted for.*

Every few seconds an opportunity for amendment.

The son, twirling his umbrella, said, "Daddy, look, if you do this it will pull you along."

The son twirling. His umbrella saying, "Look at this, man, I can pull you along."

After dinner, they went out into the rain, the three of them, and moved along the street with the rain coming down. And their umbrellas.

Thinking back, there were four ways I could've happened. One was, I might have done something and he was looking and seeing and then night falling fast with morning looking so far off. Another to do with the trees out there. A third where the cliff fell to the river.

How big was this playground thing?

Most of the time there was never anybody else on that road. There was a doctor who lived at the top of the hill. There was another house at the end of the road with a sign at the end of the drive-way.

"I seen you kids in the pond over there. Getting golf balls."

"We weren't in the pond. We were on this road."

"I seen you."

"No you never."

"What are you doing here, then? This here is private property."

"We live just over there."

"Where?"

"In the house over there."

"Well, I seen you in the pond. Getting golf balls. Stay out of the pond."

"There's a house over there."

"I know. You think I'm stupid? Nobody lives in that house. Just stay the fuck out of the pond."

I go in the bedroom. I look at the bed. I go in the bathroom. I look in the mirror. I go in the living room. I turn on the TV. Flick around. Look for something.

Ruth might be at her parents'. She goes there when I'm not home. She waits until I'm not home and then she goes there and waits till I'm home and then comes home. I could call her.

I put the volume down on the TV. Pick up a magazine. I read words. I look at the TV. A little boy is blond. He grins. Shows his mother something. The boy and the mother laugh.

I look at the magazine. I read. About elephants. In a zoo.

I look at the TV. A corpse. Hanging from a meathook. In a freezer. Two men in suits smoke. Talk. I watch. The two men talk. Smoke. Look at the corpse. I get the clicker. Turn up the volume. One man says, "Your guess is as good as mine, Roy." Commercial. I turn down the volume.

I hear a sound that sounds like it's sounding from the balcony. I look out the window. There's nothing to see but grey sky. Some cars. I look at the TV. I look at the magazine. One elephant in the story is named Pinky. Pinky dies. I picture Pinky lying on his side. His eyes closed. I close the magazine. Put it on the coffee table. Look at the TV.

The little boy and his mother are dressed in black clothes with other people dressed in black clothes all around in a place outside, a graveyard. I see this when the camera moves and shows gravestones. The two men in suits are standing away from the other people. They are talking and smoking. The camera closes on the little boy's face. He looks far away seeing something new.

He looks glad. The mother bawls her eyes out. The boy seems to not notice, hears his own something that makes him glad. The mother always bawls her eyes out, even before the person died. Now it's another reason to bawl her eyes out.

I hear the sound sound on the balcony. I get off the couch. Walk to the window. Three steps. I can see part of an arm. I open the door. Tutti. She's got a putter. She taps a golf ball. The ball rolls. Hits the rim of a juice glass. There are other balls. All around the juice glass.

"Nice try," I say.

Tutti lifts her face. Looks at me. Her eyes are red.

"What's wrong?" I say.

"I love golf," she says.

"You don't play golf."

"I could have been good. As good as Arnold Palmer. He owns dry cleaners."

"I know." I look at the sky. Clouds.

"Tim Horton owns doughnut shops."

"Tim Horton is a hockey player."

"Was he a good hockey player?"

"I don't know."

"Now he owns doughnut shops."

"He's dead."

"When did he die?"

"A long time ago."

I'm sorry, but I don't get it. I guess I never did get it. With this Lorne Lofsky guy, I never got why.

"I'm living through return of the mole people," Tutti says.

I look. I'm in the bedroom. Cleaning off my desk.

"Why don't you turn on a light?"

"Let me under there with you, Goofball," I say.

"I can't stand living with you two anymore," Tutti says. She gets a pair of socks out of her dresser and goes into the bathroom.

We get four-dollar umbrellas at Woolworths. They pop up when

44

you press a button. Tutti yells at me whenever I lose one of these umbrellas. I tell her they only cost four dollars. I tell her, "Don't yell at me." I go to the fridge to get some food. To see if there is any food. There never is, but I always find something and put it in my mouth.

That was about it. Bertrand was gone. He left. He stayed long enough to kiss June on the cheek. "If you change your mind. Call. Don't be a stranger. Can't we still be friends?" He didn't come back. He went away hurting. Like he'd been shot. But he gave it his best shot, and what more can a man do? He went for the verbal attack. He might simply have kissed her. He might have taken her to bed. He might have fallen to the floor. Clasped her knees. Begged. Instead, he went home. Got in bed. Pulled the covers up. To his chin. He didn't sleep too well. He took some pills. On the third night. He was having trouble at work. He was just too exhausted, couldn't see the bright side, only the dark underside, wondered if June had been right. That thing about escaping his dad had been the premise upon which he based everything. He felt he could not consider the possibility that he had been wrong. It would nullify his entire existence. At least he had his classical guitar training. But was that enough?

In Messier, West Virginia, six centimetres short of the dark band, the middle part of the core has two brighter portions separated by a slight darkening. The eastern lump elongated near the edge, conspicuous and larger, brightening two-thirds of the sky.

I have it in my head to do the dickens, men. Tomorrow. It cost a dollar. People say goodbye. Above the silken earth, blond about their faces. Coats covering what?
    I wanted to see. Eyes averted. Concealing light.
    I wanted to know.

Feel justified in singing. Execute the printer. Listen to their story. Especially you, Charmaine.
    Her safe arrival. Her cousins Erin, Eden and Jacob. Come

45

back to Canada, Marie. Be sent to Glebe.

No one remembers the taste of her gravy, or the size of the panties she wore, but someone swears and fifty-two years go by.

The sea is green at night, Mr. Filmore, but no one goes to the sea at night anymore. Except Sigfried. On Fridays.

I lost my pen at 4:34 p.m. I knew where it was. In a puddle. Near the curb. On Bay Street. North of Bloor. I have a gift. I know where every pen I ever owned is.

At first I thought this was cool. I told all my friends. Showed off. Threw my pens away. Dropped them into potholes. Swallowed them. Shit them out. Flushed them. Days later, I went and found them.

Then I got to wondering. Was I squandering what God had given me? Maybe I should try to use this gift. Do something good.

I went to get my pen from the puddle on Bay Street. Saw a man enter the sub shop at Cumberland. His clean well-lighted face clear of any fear. His woman passing through the sub shop door behind him.

I didn't want to hide. But every time I opened the door and uttered another useless word the man from the hide-and-glo seemed revealed. As time went on it grew. I barely spoke. When I did, I tried not to say anything writ beneath myself or deeper even.

I was so in love. When she kissed my neck it made me cry.

The man who knew smiled and shook his head to show what couldn't be.

I awoke. I was alone on the couch with gas so bad it made me cry.

The man had silver hair and kicked his heels to make us laugh. The girl was Diane and she'd brought games to pass the time. Miniature playing cards she packed away each time she saw me come. She drew pictures on her legs that I could see when her skirt fell away. Pictures and freckles on her thighs. When she kissed my mouth she put her tongue so deep I couldn't breathe.

Pictures of stick girls with sunshine hair and five-petalled flowers.

Of most concern were issues following the revelation.

Pilot from the hills: speak. That time. The still in effect. That's what I was trying for. To make clear a simple droning, they or their loss.

In Wilmet they found Lori a piano teacher. Miss Graves. Thursdays after school Lori walked four blocks south and one block west to Miss Graves' white bungalow. Lori was Miss Graves only student.

I was not angry. I was merely a place to think. By and large I am still mostly just another. I am afraid of the hard crisp languor I have seen in Myron and Otto. I am afraid of what lies beyond the flag, in the windy motion on the plane where beams of light grow hard.

I wrote what mattered. And then I wrote what didn't. In a moment I won't be capable.

"France!" she screams and France screams. Hurting looks. The empty pools of blue. Dead freesia at the bottom. She hits the window. *Slide in here*, she whispers.

The clinic will be given by Mr. Dick Lynch, Master Official. This clinic will be the last one being offered. Clinics include live demonstrations. Please note the deadline for entry. The format and the number of sessions will not be determined. Total numbers are not known. If you have worked one of two days you would be considered to have all four credits. If you have credits to make up, you must work more days. A request from you should be put in the mail slot. Please return via fax. Or e-mail. Hard copies can be dropped off. Schedules will be posted.

I was not angry. I was merely pale.

They found me in a movie. Sundays, they let me be free. When sun shone on the windows of those buildings with gold brackets, the pipe in my buttocks played *Claire de Lisa*.

Did you know they had the wake? They don't expect you in other peoples' lives. Don't make fun of me. Please. Sit down. Do you remember the fine weather we had last summer? (Naturally, I wanted to ask about his hens.) Just come over to the window, he said.

Le chasseur de bisons dut abandonner sa vie traditionelle. Contraint a adopter la façon de vivre des Blancs.

I couldn't remember if:
a) it was something I didn't want people to see me with; or
b) it was something I really didn't want.

I suggested she might be reading in a meaning that wasn't there. She said to go down to the basement, take a look around. I was doing my e-mail. I had to feed the kids. *Just go*, she said. I went down. Silence. And then the kitty litter.

Yeah, and then you come out from under the bladder hoping no one will notice. *That's what you get for living under a bladder*, she says. Her wispy hair. But if you do come out for long enough, do you heal?

Oh, you who enjoy the sun shining on your bleeding body!
We're going over to Jim's place later. Want to come?

Spot grabbed the puck. I whacked his head with my stick. "Yelp!" Spot said.
"Shut up, Spot," I said. Wind. Like a man in a plaid shirt holding me by the armpits steering me over ice.

Two kids, one of them me, one of them someone else. I want the one to be happy. The other, I don't care.

Some will use their right hand. Some still can't see it. Others covered it with leaves. Repeat with petrol, Bobby. Octans is barren. The period: 406 days.

Phoebe has shown these three are mostly due to evidence of otherwise.

"Most people," she said. And I thought I knew what was coming. Or I didn't care. A truck pulled out in front of where we were trying to get across. The driver desperate. A piece of human wreckage tipped out from a doorway. Bandage where his nose should have been. "Well," she said. "Not him."

I stand there like an idiot telling a story about Sammy. Liz keeps moving. I follow her. Keep telling my story. It's a great story. Sammy is doing something heartbreaking. It brings tears to my eyes just telling it. Liz keeps walking away. Finally, I just stand in one place. Liz moves around. Gets things done. I stand still and tell my story. And no one is listening.

One Sunday, late in the afternoon, I heard the sewing machine. I tried to go downstairs, but my feet fell like mist. I stepped outside and dreamed of cigarettes till the boys came home bigger than I'd ever seen them.

"Didn't go to work today, Dad?"

"Worried about your mother."

"Under the flaps again?" The flaps were what the boys called the white fabric flags.

"I think so."

But when the boys went down, she wasn't there. She'd vanished.

Angels again. Floating in Lake Ontario. Just off the concrete piers of Toronto. In among the litter. Every other white thing an angel. *Flotilla*, I thought, as I came back up.

There are places where he tries to tell you what he's trying to tell you. If you listen. You have to listen.

The phone rang. It was Hal. Or Lori. Or maybe Sears calling us to get a credit card. Or maybe those carpet cleaners. Or those guys who want to sell your house. Or one of those recorded messages.

The second boy was in his crib screaming. The first boy was downstairs screaming. The phone would ring. It was a tragedy.

Winners will be introduced, thanked, and awarded a prize.

I never knew what others knew.
    "I know, you know," she said.
    "I know," I said.

Best known for his 1994 bestseller: *God is in the freezer sweeping up the ice.*

He spread the cloth and ate his lunch.

All maps lead to her hole. Everything floated away.

It was hell. We ran out of food. The light was terrible for reading. Then Myron arrived.

The day is twenty-five minutes. At the end, the computers come on. You get two: before and after. From anywhere you will need. Access these machines. Click here to end session.

If I leave to make a phone call what will be lost, my darling.

The grey taskbar. The computer. Your trip to the library. Last Wednesday, over for days now.

Fire crews arrived at 5:35 a.m. Twenty minutes later, she called again.

The mantle melts just above the subducting plate. The cat fizzles.

Dear God,

How are things up there? If you know my every thought, you know I ask how things are only because I don't want you to think this letter is all about me. I want you to believe I care about you, even though you evidently don't care about me. Not the way my wife cares. She does care, by the way. Those things she does and the way she talks to me are her way of showing *just how darn much she cares!*

If you are omniscient, if you truly are the heartless, third person omniscient cad people make you out to be, it will be a waste of time to try to convince you I care how you are. I'm not stupid. I know that you just *are*, and that there is no *how* involved.

You never write, or contact me, even as a voice in my head. Too bad you don't have e-mail. You probably don't even have a computer. We've got a lot of stuff you don't have. We have cars, you bastard. You're just jealous. That's why you keep killing people. You can't stand it that we have all this stuff. And we've got it because, yes, that's right, simply because we can ask each other, "How are you?" and the question has meaning.

I really only sent this letter to you because I couldn't think of anyone real to write to. I couldn't think of anyone doomed to die who would want to read this stupid letter.

Let me start at square one, God. Down here on earth, we humans try to make believe we care about each other so that others will make believe they care back. That's why we want you to think we care about you. That's why we got so excited about Jesus, because he was someone we could care about. Ditto for Tom Cruise. Some might argue that you didn't send Tom Cruise. But — wrong! You sent everybody. Am I right?

That's all for now. I know this will take time, but I'm hoping we can become friends and that eventually you'll decide to not kill me. I'll write again soon.

P.S. I am a professional writer concerned with the questions of faith. "God's way is mysterious," they say, but they are idiots.

God has no way. I would like to call my essay: *God is killing me as we speak.*

I'm going back to Connor. I love him.

Ralph hardly heard his father's words, had no idea what they meant. He felt light pressure. His father's hand on his back. Smelled the familiar smell. Stopped crying. Lay quietly. Hoped his father would stay on the edge of the bed for a long time.

Ralph hardly heard his father. Had no idea what it meant. Felt light pressure. His father's words on his back.

Sunny beckons. "Come here." She leans forward. Pulls her hands toward her breasts. "There's something I want to show you," she says.

I load the delivery onto the flatbed. I take it to the back. The delivery guy is waiting.

"Is that for the east or the west?" the delivery guy asks. "Because if it's for the west, I'm not going to the west."

"I don't know which it's for."

"Well, I'm not going to the west."

There are feelings you can get about a person you don't spend a lot of time with that you just can't get with someone in your family.

Whenever I imagined saying things, I imagined saying them to Matty.

The delivery guy's name is Bob. He's got the tiniest eyes I've ever seen. "Just leave it," he says. "I'll check to see if it's east or west."

I go around and put toilet paper in the men's on first.

I can see where you stick the needle. And I can see where the needle comes out. But the rest is just a matter of luck.

When I go back to the workroom, Sunny is waiting. She has a videotape. It's stuck in the video machine. The flap on the video machine slot won't close. I stick my finger in. Push. Nothing.

"Oh dear," Sunny says. She puts her hands to her cheeks. Sunny is like an old lady.

I push the power button. The tape pops out. I hold the tape up. "The case is cracked," I say. I show Sunny the crack.

I hang up the phone. Go back to the table. "Mother's plane has disappeared into the Bermuda Triangle," I say.

The delivery guy is standing on the back of his truck. "This stuff is for the west." He points to a pile of boxes. "I took the stuff for the east."

"Thanks," I say. I don't mean it. I wasn't expecting the bastard to still be here.

"I forget how to work these things."

I took it. "How can you forget how to work a banana?" I peeled it. I gave her the fruit.

"Thanks."

"How old are you?"

"Twenty-three. No wait, twenty-four. Last Thursday."

"Hi. Where are you? Are you like… Where are you? At the bus stop? Are you at a bus stop? Are you bored? Are you feeling lucky? Put the book back in your purse. Have you seen the brothers? Yes, we all know. What we all know is the topic. Is often the topic. He could no longer know."

Sometimes the delivery guy comes into the delivery area with a guitar strapped around his neck. He stands in the middle of the delivery area with the guitar balanced on his stomach. He has a big stomach. He plays guitar. Sings some songs. He sings Christmas songs. No matter what time of year. He has a nice voice. Staff come back to the delivery area. Stand around the delivery guy. In a semi-circle. Sway a little. Arms crossed across their chests. It reminds me of camp. How there was always a counsellor who looked like Art Garfunkel. How that counsellor always got his guitar out every night and played and sang songs. Around the campfire. Having this camp memory makes me nauseous.

Daddy would be in the living room with his pile of books he was reading and I was his best boy.
    "You're up early." Because it is 6 a.m.
    "I couldn't sleep anymore, Daddy."
    He loved me more than life itself.

"I haven't decided. I might change my mind and never bring it up again."
    "But I already know."
    "I might eliminate you."
    "You could do that?"
    "Why not?"

This was years ago, before my father was stabbed to death. He could no longer sew buttons. His thick fingers could no longer sew. He could no longer sew. He could no longer. He could know. He could. No. He couldn't.

Then I realized the shouldliness had simply moved to sitting me at my desk. Because I should never give into the shouldliness of visiting Tutti. The never becomes the should. And now I should visit her again. These are the rounds of my visitations with Tutti.

Back in prison. Looking down at your feet. You have no shoelaces.

The unintelligible tree speaks. *Hello.* A statement against me. So. No statement at all. Tree rises from no purpose. Touches purposeless sky. Alien intelligence draws on colour. *You'll die too*, it says.

"Do you have any idea how much delivery we deliver every day?" the delivery guy asks.
    "No."

54

"Take a guess."

I shrug.

"In pounds."

"In pounds?"

"Yeah," the delivery guy says. "Go ahead. Take a guess."

"In *pounds*?" I say.

"Take a guess."

"I have no idea." I hate it when guys make you take a guess. I look at the delivery boxes piled on the floor. I scratch my chin.

"The average delivery box weighs about fifty-five pounds," the delivery guy says. "If it's full."

"Fifty-five pounds?"

"Yeah. If it's full."

I look at the boxes some more.

"Ten tons a day," the delivery guy says.

"Ten tons?" I whistle. *What a jerk. Ten tons. Fuck you.*

Once I was playing in my backyard. I was lonely. I said, "I wish I had a friend to play with." Just then, something startled me! A Grizzly Bear had climbed over the fence. "Oh no!" I said. "I've got to tell my mom," I said. It ran after me into the house. My mom was sewing. She said "HELP HELP!!" Me and mom yelled to all of the people in the town. But then the Grizzly Bear fell down. Then we lived happily ever after.

-by Shortboy.

If a rose is a rose by any other name, then a stranger is a stranger, even if he tells you he's your dad.

Kowalski is dead. Drowned. Florida. His brother, Tom, tried to save him. Tom swam out to where Kowalski was. But Kowalski was gone. He washed up on shore next day. A priest found him.

Sometimes I'm surprised I lived. You hear about people shooting each other. Dying in cars.

I ran into Kowalski's mother in Shoppers Drug Mart once not

long ago. She tried to hug me. Kowalski probably thought he would get down to Florida and hook up with some women. I don't know what he thought.

A guy came running up to my car and made me roll down my window. He made me give him my driver's licence. He took my driver's licence and read the number into a tape recorder.

Kowalski's sisters had bad teeth. They wore capes. They came to our high school dance once. They'd both been out of high school for years. Kowalski had the same black hair as them. You could see the dandruff. One of the sisters died. Leukemia.

"I was going north, northwest when I hit you," I said to the girl when I got out of my car. The girl stood by her car. She had to squint. The sun. In her eyes. "These compass things don't do a bit of good," I said. "My wife laughed when I came home with this compass on the dashboard. She thought it was funny. But it isn't."

I picked up the phone. The cord was frayed. *This phone won't last much longer*, I thought. *One day it won't work. Say you have to buy a dozen new phones in your lifetime. Each phone breaks. You find out it can't be fixed. So you buy a new one. Say each phone costs a hundred bucks. So what?*

I called the police. Went downstairs. The house was dark. There was one ray of light. It shone through the window above the door. This ray of light shone like a spotlight in a dark theatre. It struck one of the stairs on the staircase. I had to pass right through it to get to the kitchen. I intended to make myself a cup of coffee. This seemed like a good idea. This cup of coffee. All the way down the stairs I thought about this. I decided to make a full pot. I would offer a cup to the police officer when he arrived. I imagined he would be young, with fresh skin, and sympathetic to my plight.

He gets the basketball right away. None of this will make any sense. What I'm trying to tell you is, I know what comes after the cows and the cream-coloured bands and the moment when Cal gets his fly unzipped. I know what comes next. The way she sat. Dabbing her eyes. Her eyes all red. Like she was crying. But it was the wind. They had to stop because of the wind. It's that kind of life now, for her. Things lift things up in the wind. Wind lifts things it never lifted before. One day, if it gets strong enough, the wind will lift her. It might never set her down.

A woman might want to be filled. Sometimes everything seems possible. Wind blew curtains into the room. I saw the sky. Some clouds. I heard a lawn mower. Somewhere. Not far off. The lawn mower stopped. I heard car tires. In the street. Below the window. The lawn mower started up again.

"I then kill Bowser and cut off his wiener and cut it in half and eat it. And you know what my sauce is? Pee. And then I cut out his teeth and they're huge and the tooth fairy gives me fifty million dollars."

I remember the smell of sleep in the boys' room at night. The two of them lying silent, bodies spread strangely over covers, window open. The air uniquely theirs — close, but somehow young. Age would erase it.

They slept in the same room till Milo was 14, Carter 10. Telling whispered jokes till Leila told them to pipe down.

He pulled the boy up onto the back of the horse and cantered out through a back gate the boy hadn't known of, in spite of all the times he'd visited the cemetery.

"Where are we going?" the boy asked into the stranger's back. He smelled the man's leather. The man's smoke.

"We'll get something to eat, I believe," the man said, as though he wasn't quite sure where he was going, but not uncertain at all, more like he was certain he'd never know where he was going. "Food seems like a good idea right now," he continued. "Don't you think?"

"Sounds good to me," said the boy. The boy didn't care. Anything sounded good to a boy his age.

They rode the sidewalk. Occasionally a car passed by on the street, headlights illuminating the shanks of the horse and the boots of the rider and nothing of the boy behind. If anyone took exception to the fact of a horse in this modern-day residential neighbourhood, you'd never know it. *But then*, thought the boy, *how would we know? How would we know anything? What is there to know?*

They emerged into an open space and the man brought the horse up short on a hill of brown dusty grass. Trees long gone. The man hooked the boy under his arms and lowered him to the ground, leaning low over the right side of the horse. The horse stamped once and blew air. The skin under its main quivered and it lowered its long face to the ground, snuffled the dirt. The boy's feet settled not far from the horse's face. His back to horse and man, the boy gazed over the scorched country.

"Smoke," said the boy in a voice like smoke. Thick. Rattling. Some ailing creature crawling out from his belly. He spoke so quietly that the man would not have heard had he not been leaning close to where he deposited the boy a moment before. The old man kicked a foot over the back of the horse and stepped down out of the saddle, set his tired self down onto the ground next to the boy. One of the stirrups shimmered in the blinding sun. The man stood beside and above the boy and together they looked at the smoke. The man saw in that smoke many writhing possibilities, each threading a different way, each finding its own vaporous end in the blinding blue of the sunlit sky. What the boy saw was something the man could hardly discern, for he had begun to feel that the boy felt nothing akin to what he himself felt. The old man saw in the boy only an opportunity, an emptiness that called for filling in in a way the man could hardly resist.

Fluffy eats plants. She especially likes the ones that hang above the back of our couch. We call those plants the vegetable patch. Fluffy likes to chew on the plant called Hairy. You can water Hairy every day and he never dies. If you sit on the couch, Hairy gets in your eyes. We don't care. Hairy is the only plant we have that's never died. All the other plants are dead.

The man knocked and the boy stood back of and beside the man, as though things had been arranged ahead of time, as though the man and the boy had discussed the matter and come to some understanding. But, if what followed was preordained in any manner — if the relentlessly heavy toppling of one event onto another was irreversibly preconfigured — it was so only in the way a cloud reconfigures in wind. For, in fact, man and boy had not spoken a word since the boy saw the smoke and stamped it with its whispery moniker.

I was around ten when I got Fluffy. Now I'm 28. I'm married. Fluffy lives with me and my wife. In our apartment. Fluffy goes out on the balcony sometimes. Licks things. The grey bricks I've got piled out there. I was probably going to build something sometime. My wife thinks there's some deficiency in Fluffy's diet.

"A brick deficiency?" I ask. I shake my head. My wife and I are standing at the window. Inside the apartment. In the living room. We're looking out at the balcony. Watching Fluffy lick bricks.

The strange man sat on a metal pipe that left the ground at an angle and stopped, capped, about two feet up. No apparent reason for a pipe, nor a strange man sitting atop a pipe, but the boy tugged at the old man's sleeve and they stopped. The strange man wore black socks stretched to his knees. His shorts stopped midway along his thighs. His thighs were skinny. They dangled over the brown grass like bent or broken bulrushes. The strange man wore a dirty woollen tam that might have been yellow at one time, with a pompom so red it seemed an afterthought, and, indeed, must have been added after. The strange man's eyes glowed like coals inside their deep dark sockets, but the strange man's brow was smooth and unworried.

"Let's take him with us," whispered the boy into the old man's back.

"He'll slow us down."

"I want him to come."

The strange man looked up when he heard the hushed voices. He smiled benignly, but seemed to know what they were saying, for he stood suddenly and strode off quite quickly on his spindly legs.

Does a whale have a combination of food choices and self-esteem that affect its body weight? Some people say no, but I think it does. I support this opinion by saying that people who see a lot of TV have seen a lot of whales, but these are whales on TV. This will happen mostly in urban parts of the world. It will affect mostly adults, but those adults may have had an experience in their childhood. This experience may have involved thin models and actors on commercials with jingles and pictures. Sometimes the commercials do not have actors and models, but they have a way of making the food look delectable or healthy.

I have shown that because whales are mainly on TV, particularly in urban areas, we are often influenced in ways we cannot control.

God only forgives those who… I can't remember.

The thing Jane thought she was slithering toward fades and Jane stands up. She thinks she has been asleep. It is 3 a.m. Jane goes to the window. Across the street, there are the other houses.

Anytime I hear the saxophone, I think of Dad. I think, *Dad would have liked that one.* But he wouldn't have. He wouldn't have liked any of them. Who knew what Dad liked? Who knows what anyone would like. I don't.

I know what Mom likes. Mom likes TV shows.

Maybe it goes *God never forgives those who…* Something.

When she died, I regained my wholeness. I have been whole ever since. She was the miracle cure the doctors never mention anymore.

I decided I should try to drive all the way. I got in the car. I started the motor. I drove for half an hour. I was looking for a doughnut shop. Someplace to get a coffee. I stopped at a gas station. They sold chocolate bars.

"What happened?"

"I made your lunch. It's in the fridge." She rolls over. Closes her eyes.

There is a woman at work who works on the same memo every day. She tries to make it better. Better and better. I ask her to show it to me.

"There is no memo," she says. "There never was." She is twenty-eight years old. "I'm never having children," she tells me. "I have a dog. A dog is enough." She drives a Volvo with a wire barrier behind the driver's seat where she keeps the dog.

I don't see anything anymore.

I can see the words on the page in front of me.

I didn't say it like that. I didn't say it like anything.

Two days now.

Mom will die.

I will die.

Those men in hats will die.

I think they're going to bury the men in hats over there.

I put on my sunglasses.

I call Phillip.

He puts me on hold. Comes back on. "Go home," he says.

After I got in bed, I remembered the little blue flowers Sammy had picked. "I'm picking them for Mommy," he said.

Those flowers were still in the car. I couldn't go to sleep. I was thinking about the flowers. I went to sleep. I woke up. It was time to go to work again.

He got the carrots out. The carrots were in a bag. I guess that's about it. I guess that's about all that matters. The carrots. In a bag.

It was him who got the carrots out. He got them out of the bag. He got the bag open. He got the carrots out. He pulled each carrot out.

In the car, on the way home, he said, "We should buy a fireplace. We need to get a little carrot for Rudolph and a big carrot for Rudolph's daddy, Daddy."

I knew things ahead of time. I wanted people to tell me something. I was waiting for someone. What were people going to tell me?

We got coffee on my lunch hour. Dad didn't work. Hadn't worked in years. By the time the second one came, I was running out of words. I lay on the floor with my eyes closed. I get up. Go up the stairs. Out the door. I stand on the porch. Wind.

It's okay. I saw them yesterday. Doing that thing they do. I saw the cats. Tell them I saw the cats. Tell them it's 8:30 in the morning here.

John drove a truck. Big rig. Knew nothing about the thing. Knew how to drive it. Double shift. Brake. Red light. Green light. Town. Highway. The other truckers knew their rigs. The other truckers knew their rigs better than they knew their women. They knew what was inside their rigs. What's inside a woman?

When the fridge comes on, Jane knows this is her cue. She ascends the first of the fourteen steps to the upper level. She cannot yet be sure where this will lead. Although it's a safe bet it will be somewhere upstairs.

They need salt and a thousand other ingredients if ever they are going to make that dish they've longed so long to make. If you long for something in the first week you get married, and then go on longing for it through years of marriage — not pickles, but like that, something with oregano, but that's all that can be said — does the quality of longing change with the length of time you long? Does the object for which you long really change? Is longing a way of practising for death? Or is longing a way of cheating death? Is longing the shape of hope? Does the grandchild open his mouth on hope? Does hope open a mouth itself, like the sound of conversation in the middle of the busiest day?

The train goes by our apartment at night. Some night it will stop and let someone off. Someone a lot like Jesus Christ, only better. Someone in charge of everyone. Someone a lot like Miss Vivian, my Grade 2 teacher.

We must have made some kind of mistake. It must have been a bad mistake. It must have been some crazy thing. Something we needed to get out of our system.

One day when he's old, he'll find that book lying on a wooden table in a store in New York City. He won't be reading anything at the time. The book will be a deal. He'll buy it. He'll tell himself, *This can't be the book I saw so many years ago.* But as he reads, he'll go back to the day he first saw the book. He'll lose himself. Relive his childhood. Back up. He'll know that when he finishes the book, he will die. His death with be simultaneous with the turning over of the back cover of the book. He'll die in that chair he sits in after dinner, the book upside down in his lap. People will find him and smile, hoping for a death as painless, as fraught with meaning, as his.

The hunter in this story is the need to drive us toward a conclusion by projecting larger and larger manifestations of the same thing. This is the popular notion of story, and it is because of this notion that biographers can categorize a person, like, for instance, that guy I read about who was self-destructive and drove himself into a deeper and deeper hole. If this were true — but it isn't, so why speculate.

Jane laughs. James laughs. He gets a new idea about the peas. "Maybe she is a bitch," he says. "But the husband likes her." He hears a voice in her head. Eats his noodles and his slice of bread.

Say he lost his keys, though. Say he looked everywhere. Checked his pockets. Looked on the tables.

You can't absorb anything else. Today it is so bad you are having trouble absorbing anything but this lady's nipples. When you were a kid, you'd get a hard-on just looking at topless women. Now you just stare and marvel at how far newspapers have come. You wish you could maybe get a little hard-on, just for old times sake. You ask your dick: "What have we come to?" You laugh. You chuckle softly to yourself when you realize you are having a conversation with your dick. You try to keep the conversation going. You try having a conversation with your knee.

There was a woman down in the subway. It was March. Outside the snow was blowing. The women's children were dancing. One child, a girl with short hair like a boy, was dancing backward along the subway platform. Already, the mother had taken these children a long stretch further on this journey than she ever intended.

He missed the flight out of Chicago. He stood in the observation lounge and watched the plane he was supposed to be on taxi out to the runway. Then he watched it take off.

When he was a youth living with his mother, he once put his fist through his bedroom door. And he knew a man who broke all his fingers punching a concrete wall.

She was my editor. Everybody was my editor. After we fucked, she asked me questions. "What was that place — it was in that movie we saw?"
    "What place? What movie?"
    She was drinking something through a straw.

She worries that the buildings aren't where they should be.

Underneath my feet were steps made of little stones. Little stones that they'd cemented together.

"Who cemented them together?"

"The people who made the building."

"Who made it?"

"I don't know. This is about the little stones. Not who made the building."

"Are you saying I don't need to know who made the building?"

"Yes, that's what I'm saying."

"You're sure I don't need to know?"

"I'm positive. It's just about the little stones."

"Okay. Go on."

Underneath my feet were steps made of little stones. Little stones cemented together. I thought, *Where did they get all those little stones?*

"You see?"

"What?"

"It would help to know who *they* are. Don't you think? You keep mentioning them. I would help to know what they look like."

"I don't know what they look like. I don't know who they are. There's a lot of them. You don't get one or two people building steps like that. You get a construction company. You get an architect. There's the workers and the bosses and the secretaries back at the office taking calls and the truck drivers and the men in the quarry where the little stones are harvested."

"That helps."

"I don't see how that could help."

"It does. Now go on."

Underneath my feet were steps made of little stones. Little stones cemented together. I thought, *Where did they get all those little stones?* I had my lunch with me. In a brown bag. I was trying to remember what I'd put in my lunch that morning. I took a look around. To my right, there was a whole building made of little stones. *There mustn't be any little stones left,* I thought. *They've used up all the little stones. Why would they build a whole build-ing out of those little stones? Why would they do that?* I thought about my lunch again.

What is the shape of the space inside a word? When you bring the shape of the space inside the word to the word, what does the other bring? If you already hear the shape of the space inside the word, even before the other speaks the word, what can the other ever hope to bring you?

Walk 50 paces. When you see a river, turn into the wood and continue on to the biggest boulder. I've left you a package by the boulder.

The message was etched in rock. The man who carved the message was long since dead. The intended recipient — also dead. The package was still by the boulder.

"It's a message," said the man on the horse.

"What's it say?" said the other.

"Don't know," said the man on the horse.

Neither man could read.

He threw out most of what he wrote, but he kept every shopping list he ever made.

I come home after work. Tutti has her sewing machine pulled apart. Lying in pieces. On the table. In the kitchen. Tutti is crying. She is sitting at the kitchen table with pieces of her sewing machine spread out around her and she is crying. She opens her mouth. A little sob comes out. Her eyes make me think of an animal. An animal that has been shot, but hasn't fallen. An animal standing in the vast damp forest waiting to fall.

I had to go to this meeting, so I got on my bicycle. I knew I'd get there early. I went down Bathurst Street to Wilson and across Wilson to Keele. I had to pass the place where my dad used to have his store.

When Tutti and I were making arrangements to get married, we went to Piper Studios. Tutti was looking for a wedding dress and I was going around to the various stores with her. Sometimes her parents came. I would hang around. In the mall. At the water fountain. At the food court. In the car sometimes. Tutti tried on dresses. This was a sad time in my life.

He's outside the house. He's looking for a way in. The most direct way.

When Dad phoned to tell me he had cancer, I can't remember what he said, except one thing I remember him saying was, "It isn't fair."

On weekends I take off my watch. I put it back on Monday mornings.

The things I want are, first of all, Laine.
    Laine likes books. She likes books better than she likes me. When Laine sees me, she sees the possibility of books.
    I drop in on Laine. Briefly. I lend her a book. Then I get out. I tell myself, *Laine is busy. I shouldn't keep her.*

The books are a way into another place. A way out of this place. Or a way back into this place. A better entrance. A manner of transformation. A manifestation. This place as a place I hadn't considered.

"What are you doing here?" Laine asks.
    I show her the book I want to lend her.
    "You shouldn't be in here," she tells me. Her voice is hollow from the tiles on the walls. The washroom is dark, with unexpected spots of light.
    Laine takes the book. She looks at the cover. A naked man, his cock limp, his head bent, his chest caved over his stomach, the hair on his head falling. Laine opens the book.

When I find a book that makes a clear view into a place I want to be, I go there to that place, but then, it is never enough. It is never enough to go to the place the good books take me without wanting to take myself to that place again when the book has left me.

I step back, close the book.

Have I left the place? Have I left that good place the good book takes me? Did I ever leave the place I was actually in and go to another place, a good place the good book could take me? Did I ever really go to the new place I thought I could go to through the book? Was I ever really in the place I was in? Was there ever a place to be in? Where am I before I read a book? Where am I after? Where is it that I so desperately want to take myself when I read a book?

I was dancing in the rain. I put bags on my shoes to keep them dry, but my shoes got wet. It was raining and then it was snowing and then it stopped and just a cold wind blew and it was dusk, almost dark, and I could see the red sky in the west where the sky was clearing. I got off my bike in a park and I took the bags off my shoes and threw the bags in the garbage. Then I took my shoes and socks off and stood on the cement path in the park in my bare feet and I rolled my pants up to keep them out of the chain. I stuck my wet socks in the bag on the back of my bike and put my bare feet into my shoes and got on my bike.

One thing for sure, I want to go back.

Laine hands me back the book. She looks me in the eye. Her eyes are small and her hair is cut in a pageboy. She must see something in my eye she doesn't want to see because she looks away. "You shouldn't be in here," she says.

If I ever manage to linger in the place I want to be long enough to make some record of it, I'll be so far gone, no one will ever catch up. I'll be so close to death, you'll taste it in everything I say. I'll jump back before it kills me, but I won't jump back so far that I can't turn and face it again, anytime — anytime I want.

If I get to that place I'm wanting to go, I'll be entirely alone. I've been there actually. I know I've been there because of how alone I've felt. It's hard to feel that alone. When I feel that alone, I want to come back, to have friends, to talk to people about nothing that matters. But I want to stay alone, too. I want, it seems, to find a way to be that alone in the presence of others.

I had finished high school a long time ago. I tried to imagine how it would have been if I had gone to high school at a different time.

At its best, poetry causes a group of words to congregate around their hopeless appeal to hope. Words have no appeal one to the other in poetry, only the unexpected discovery that they have become one among many and that the accident of meaning looms, always imminent.

How I picture it is, the guy is up on the toilet seat with his bare bum against the wall. The girl is standing on the floor.

It means: You are at the end of it all before you even get started. It's the same as you can't ever catch yourself by surprise looking in the mirror.

As I pick up my book, I know something. Each time I pick up my book, I know. I have knowledge. Un-deconstructable knowledge. Knowledge that fully resists analysis. Carnal in that respect. At best, I can muster a temporary bravado concerning this knowledge, a false platform above the abyss constructed of the knowledge that I can never know. I can fake it with conviction for a time, in other words. I can stand. Walk. Polish an apple. Even take that first bite.

I would say the funniest part of all of this is — and I can laugh now because I've got people around me who love me and I've got Tutti's shirt on and I can smell the armpits — is that Gary is downtown sleeping in a building where they carry guns. And that poor bastard David from Ohio. David should go back to Ohio. The poor sonofabitch. He should go back.

He drank a lot of milk, they say.

She looked into the firmament
and asked me what was permanent.
I said, "It doesn't matter."
Said, "Grandma had a platter
she used to like to eat off,
but now I have to beat off
the people who were stranded
the day that moonship landed."

I believe that everything is an opportunity. I realized this when I was playing tennis with Dad. Every time the ball came back to me, I thought, *This is an opportunity*.

Raj keeps talking about traffic, even though her mind is on something she thinks is more important. As she talks about traffic, she touches her chin and tries to pinpoint whatever it is that's driving her crazy.

Lisa keeps concentrating on traffic, thinking up different things to say about traffic, but what her mind is on, actually, is photocopying. She has a great deal of photocopying to do. It's a complicated job, involving two-sided copying and stapled sets. Lisa is on a deadline.

Raj is trying to think up more things to say about traffic. She is trying to flood her mind with things about traffic. Her stories about traffic have an edge of desperation. Every now and then she sees something that looks like it is red. It looks like it is emanating from the photocopier. Now Raj begins to talk about traffic as though her life depended on it.

"I find if I eat something while driving it helps," Lisa says. She knows that if she can get this photocopy job done right, she will be okay.

There was nothing down there, but we kept looking anyway. I don't know what the cat was thinking. I was thinking that this apartment building was getting rundown. It was okay when

I first moved in. It didn't seem so bad. But now I was married. I had a cat.

I always understood school for what it was. A place where all the kids went, where you kept going until you were eighteen, possibly twenty-five. I never believed it would do me any good. I always felt doing good was a thing I'd have to do alone.

There were things that were beginning to matter in life that had never mattered before. I got all the towels. I got the green rug off the bathroom floor. There were little hard gravel-like things falling off the rug. I could hear them hitting the hardwood floor. Downstairs, I turned on the washing machine. I listened for things happening in the house.

There are no colours left for the person who considers suicide. No blue, blue sea. No mild green grass. No mildness of any kind. No savagery either. No deep, deep heartfelt understanding of the world of adjectives.

Kerry is dead now. He died in the water in Florida on spring break one year. Danielle called me at work to tell me. I worked at McDonalds. I was standing in the back room squirting ketchup onto burgers. When I got off the phone, I went back to squirting. It's what you do. I saw no way clear of it. No way clear of anything. I tried to estimate the correct behaviour. Always. And if I couldn't? I became frightened.

We were sleeping in a park in Vancouver. At one end of the park was the ocean. All night we heard waves slapping logs. The sky was perfect. We lay on our backs. Saw stars. Everything was huge. I fell asleep. I dreamed that buildings were falling. I could hear dust rising where buildings had collapsed.

The major limitation on research based on secondary data has to do with the availability and completeness of the data. I can't get the vertical blinds to go straight. My mother has been washing her hair in the kitchen sink for twenty minutes. All our appliances are white.

I bought one of those compasses you put on your dash. I put the compass on my dash and went downtown. I moved the car around the streets. Watched the compass change directions.

I look out the window at the clouds. There are fluffy white clouds out there, with blue sky painted all around. We are alone in our bedroom. The woman is sleeping. I hear air coming out of her nose. The plan has been to take a nap. We will both go to sleep. We will both wake up. We will feel better. When the boy awakes, we will feel refreshed. Renewed.

I have one last thing to tell you. That will be it. I won't have anything more to say. This last thing that I tell you, it will be something special. It will be as special as a river. It will take me the rest of my life to say it. It will be as special as a river.

It always sounded to me like that guy was starting over.

"When do you want to get your hair cut?"
  "Thursday. At 9:30."

Everything in the city was dead. She liked the garbage. She liked the way it rolled across the dead grass in the hot wind.

It's funny how sad you get sometimes. Sometimes it seems like your sadness is all you've got. You're lying on the bed. You can't raise your arms. You are a guy on a bed who can't raise his arms.

Ron walked down the steps. The fat guy was coming up.
  "Hi, Ron," the fat guy said.
  "Hi, fat guy," Ron said.

We all long for hotdogs. Birch trees. Parked cars. I watched the sunset. I tried to keep the swear words off my lips. The air was hot. You could smell the air. The air smelled hot. Kids smelled like air. And throwup. I ate my dinner and rushed out the door. Still in my suit. I had no time. I drove slowly. Always watching the stop signs. At the last stop sign, I sat for a while. I remembered other stop signs I had beaten.

"I don't want to go in." I stood outside. Inside, there were a lot of people. Outside, I stood. I didn't want to go in. "Let's not go in," I said.

I ran out of the place and stood in the street and looked. It rose up toward the sky. It was brown. And vast. Inside we had a circular staircase. I got out my phone.

Getting up in the morning. The earth rotating.

One morning, I got out of bed. I started to pack a bag. *You need a horse*, said the voice.

This is me. This is you. Here you are beside me. Here I am ahead of you. There we are by a sparkling something.

Got married. Had kids. Was driving a little import. But it wasn't big enough for all our stuff.

Earlier, Sammy had said to me: "You know what I wish, Daddy? I wish Blanky and Doggy could come alive. Maybe I'll ask Santa to make them come alive."

Every night, before he goes to bed, Sammy tells Muggins, "I have to go to bed now, but I'll see you in the morning," and he squats down and pats Muggins on the head. Muggins is the size of a cat.

Sammy didn't like to be left alone, so when I went out for ice, he wanted to come along. On the elevator, a bald man got on with a blonde woman who had hair like rope. The bald man looked at us defiantly. The blonde woman looked at the bald man. She held his arm. Looked at the side of his face. He looked at us. There was also a man from Ohio on the elevator. When the elevator stopped, me and Sammy and the man from Ohio got off to see if the ice machine on this floor was working.

From upstairs, James begins his descent. *I married a woman named Jane*, he thinks. Next door there is the white wooden house with the concrete addition. Next to the house with the concrete addition is the house where they don't cut the grass. Next to that is the house with the willow tree and all the grandchildren.

After a while, whenever I dressed Sammy, he'd ask me if I was sure the things I put on him went together.
    "Green!" I'd say. "Everything's green!"
    "What about the socks?" he'd ask.
    I'd go and find a pair of green socks.

I was up by the bedroom cupboard where I keep my clothes and I was taking off my clothes and going over to the bed to get my PJs out from under the pillow where they're kept days while I'm at work and I had all my clothes off, I was naked, walking toward the bed and really exhausted, I just wanted to fall on the bed and lie there with my facial muscles slack, drool trickling from my mouth, and I thought, *I don't care if I die right now.*

The many different faces of death. Some days — about one out of every hundred or so — I really don't care if I die. Most days, death scares me.

It's about the secret life of malls. You know. The place where the ugliness — I'm talking now about the girls in gold tops with high heels and perfect skin and big chests — that ugliness sits out right beside the place that sells muffins. With the plastic muffin showcase. Scratched up now after all these years. So the muffins look blurry. And the taste of the muffins is fat. The rolls of fat around the waists of the women pushing strollers. Even out in the parking lot. The ugliness. And then, on the street, in the subdivisions that surround the mall, right up until the moment I lose consciousness.

Dad's face never lost its youthful appearance. On the last day of his life, his face fell apart, but it never actually looked old. It looked retarded.

What the hell was I thinking?

He maundered through the world like a poor television signal, like something fading in and out, now and then threatening coherence.

"Time to get up."
   "What are you doing?"
   "Getting up."
   "I can get up."
   "Stay."
   "I don't want the kittens to get us up earlier and earlier every morning."
   "Okay."
   Tutti got back in bed. Put her head on my arm. Cars outside the window. A radio.
   "The paper guy."
   "Fuck."
   I got out of bed. Opened the door. The kittens broke in. Tutti got out of bed.
   "What are you doing?"
   "Getting up."
   "Why?"
   "I'm not tired."
   "What are you going to do?"
   "Go downstairs."
   I went downstairs. I could hear Tutti. The kittens.

He never wore dirty socks. I know. I always noticed that. I always looked at him. At his ankles. Whenever he went by. I always said

75

to myself, *That guy never wears dirty socks.* And they were always white socks. Always. With shorts. You could see his socks perfectly because he always wore shorts. Incredible. That's what made him okay in my books. There are people who don't care about their socks.

"You need a haircut."
    "I don't want a haircut today."
    "When, then?"
    "Thursday, Daddy. At 9:30."
    The hairdresser filed her nails. They were red.

The kids ran upstairs. They went into Sammy's room. Sammy closed the door. The shelves in John and Ruth's room came down. On the shelves were Ruth's trinkets. Ruth and John got up from the table. "What was that?" John called. The boys didn't answer. John climbed the stairs. Ruth followed. Ruth's Mickey and Minnie statues were in pieces. Mickey's hands were on opposite ends of the room. His head was under the blue stool the boys used to reach things that were too high for them to reach. The little blown glass whales that the boys had given Ruth one year for Christmas — their tails in places around the room a far distance from their bodies. Things had flown apart upon impact. John went for the broom. Ruth didn't move. John returned. Ruth still in the doorway. John swept the pieces into a dustpan. Ruth left. Went downstairs. The boys came to see. "What happened?" "The shelf fell." The boys went back to Sammy's room. Closed the door again. Shortboy opened the door and came out "I think Sammy did it." "Nobody did it. The shelves just fell." "I think Sammy slammed the door." "I did slam the door." "Why did you slam the door?" "I didn't mean to." "The shelves just fell. Forget about it. Play." The boys left. John dumped the bits of ceramic and glass into the garbage pail. He could hear Ruth putting dishes in the sink. Rinsing them. Running water to wash dishes. John picked a yellow foot out of the garbage. He picked out a pink hand. He put these on the bed. He took piece after piece out of the garbage. When there was nothing but crushed powder left, he set the garbage pail down. He gathered up the pieces. Took them to the basement. He got some glue. Everything went together except for Mickey's left ear. There were white streaks on his ear where it had broken into three pieces. His right ear was intact. John got black paint from the kids' craft box. He painted over the white parts on Mickey's ear. He took Mickey and Minnie and the whales upstairs. Put them on Ruth's dresser. Went downstairs. Ruth was finished washing dishes. She put the dish towel on the hook. The boys came downstairs. They went out together into the hot summer evening to see if they could find something fun to do.

Later in the day the air warmed up. Other people came out. The beach got busy. There were flies.

In class, one of the students, a girl named Pretty, reads a story about meeting up with her sisters at the hospital on the day her father dies. When she stops reading, everybody compliments her. People say things like: "It's the most moving story I've heard all year." Or: "I was almost in tears."

Then Beth, our workshop leader, says: "It's fine to say you love a story and it's the best one yet. We seem to keep doing that. I think the story has a lot of flaws. The narrator acts too superior to her sisters." She says some other things to back up her point.

"I think you're dead wrong," someone named Chuck says. "I think the story was great. The narrator was honest. Nothing in the story should be changed."

Someone named Glinda says: "The first time through, you get so caught up in the story that you don't notice any problems. On the second reading, though, you see there are flaws."

Someone — Elron — says: "The narrator is too cruel to the sister who can't have children. I wouldn't be that cruel. It isn't human nature."

"I bought these things in China," Dustin says. He holds the things up in front of my face. "I was in China last year."

I look at Dustin. Not because I think he's nuts, or stupid, or because I loathe and despise him. I want to see if he says any more. If he wants to say more, I'll listen. I'm open to hearing more.

But Dustin has nothing more to say. I look at him until he grows uncomfortable and goes away.

I'm having an adventure when Tutti wakes me up.

"You were dreaming."

The girl in the dream was naked. I can't remember what lent everything that glow, or how these brilliant-edged disks got under my eyelids.

"Was I the girl again?" Tutti asks. "Was I naked?"

I nod, but it's dark and I don't think she can see.

"Dogs shouldn't be allowed to run free."

"Carry a gun."

"Don't be an asshole."

"Carry a club."

"People should keep their dogs on a leash. We were talking about it at work. One lady has a dog and she's still afraid of other people's dogs. She doesn't trust them."

"   "

"I had the worst sleep last night. I kept waking up afraid. And I was sweating like a pig."

"We could open the window."

"It was too cold last night. We gotta put a sheet on that bed."

I helped Katy unpack boxes of brochures and then repack them into bundles of 700.

Melissa came up while I was heading away from the brochures on a washroom break. There are things I don't see and I could knock myself for missing them, but the whack they give me when I finally cotton on is pure delight. Melissa said something weird just happened.

The block is good. But the spear is better.

That's good stuff.

I didn't expect an alien. Dodododododododo.

Look! You broke it. Where was that piece? You broke it. I don't think it was, but that might have been you.

That was me.

Bang. Crash. Bang crash. Bangcrash.

Ahhhh — it broke.

You can make your own town.

Nobody can take the sword.

A-ha, I'll get the sword. What! It doesn't work!

I'm bringing an axe then.

I'm putting it in here.

Zzzzzzt.

Oh no, oh no, help me, help me, help me.

I'll bring a spear.

Oh no.

I'm bringing the sword.

Oh no! It's gonna get stuck.

Help, I'm trapped, I'm trapped.

Jump.

You can put this on backwards.

No way.

Tell me.

Longer. The longer the better. I like this one.

Dun dun dun dun dun.

Him facing with nothing.

Drat.

Gengar.

But that's just my old one. You thought this was my new one. But it isn't. It's my old one. It's supposed to be like that.

I don't need a shield. All I need is two swords.

No you don't.

Yes I do. Because I like two. I don't know which one is best. But let's FIND OUT!

That didn't even hurt me.

Okay. Take THIS!

Thank you for more power.

At night it's just like we're at home, with Mark asleep and Mary

79

asleep on the couch and all you hear is one dog barking and the waves rolling over themselves and landing on the beach.

Getting up in the morning had become a feminist gesture. Meanwhile, the earth, rotating in the blinking permanence of the firmament, had become a condemnation.

This is me. This is you. Here you are beside me. Here I am ahead of you on the road. There we are by a sparkling something. Something is sparkling.

Alfred is crying. A tear slides over his cheek toward his ear. *Why do they go toward my ear?* he wonders. On the computer screen in front of him: text for an article about recent heat alerts. Saving the lives of old people. *I'm one of those old people*, Alfred thinks. *I cry. I don't get my work done. I get assignments of no consequence. I save old people by heat alerts.* Alfred rises up out of himself to become something more like the self he knows himself to be. Sadder in a more accomplished — a much more complicated — manner.
    Everything in the article about heat alerts is, amazingly, spelled correctly.

The list of existing things is endless. Anne Carson pretty much proved that already. She listed the major things and the minor things. Some of the major things and some of the minor things. But she pointed out that, in the end, the list itself is endless. Pretty much, anyway.

The list of existence is endless, she said. Who was she? Was she as fat as all that?

Gaze upon them as if, for once, they weren't some projection of you. I have to prove that the call to review is not influenced by the promise to improve. Who is the *they* who is making you a liar.

One night, I was walking home from the bus after work. It was a beautiful warm night. With a breeze. I saw a man walking.

Enjoying the air. I thought of myself walking. I tried to think of the last time I'd walked along like that man. Just enjoying the air. *It must have been just before I hurt my back*, I thought. But it wasn't. I'd always been rushing around before that. Trying to get to wherever it was I was trying to go. So it must have been when I was in my twenties. Or my teens. But that was wrong. I always had my head full of something back then. Some plan. Some concern. In the end, as near as I could figure it, I decided it must have been when I was a kid around two or three years old. Not that I could remember that far back. But that's just it. It must have been back before I could remember.

The rug was green. He went up the stairs. Two cats looked at him. He put his bowl and mug on the counter. The cats were there. They were his children's cats. He knew that. He remembered when the children got them. A year ago. He went downstairs. He sat in a chair. He got out of the chair. *What time is it?* he wondered. He picked up three bags. Went outside. His bike would be in the garage. It was there last night. It was there the day before.

Well, I said, they stole my dad away is what they did. What *them* would tell you. First Man: who lost him, then determined he was to be lost to us all. When it came time to bury the ashes he landed like something loosed from the wind.

The poems start off to be about something, but the wind ups and brings them to nothing in the yaw of desire.

Where would you get a bulb like that? He pulled the plug. Got off the bed. Walked. A doorway. The bathroom. Another doorway. Another bed. His. He put the book light on the bedside table. Looked. Turned off the lamp. Rolled on his side. Closed his eyes.

Prairie Fire reeks. It is big. It is shiny. And it sponsors contests.

Whereas, we want to see each human motion encompass all that life could mean. Each step. Each flickering eye. Things in blocks — family, home, money, work, space, theory. At issue is the definition of what human motion would be in a society freed from capitalist exploitation and the alienation it engenders on all levels of social organization. The boy who sweeps the curb passes the car of the boy who didn't shave. The girlfriend beholds the face not shaved.

When Oliver Reed died while making *Gladiator*, men in Hollywood were secretly awed.

We made the walls only to find the shadows made by the walls.

The leaves fall further, like dancers unhinged from thought, reasons for wind. The old man watches, hunkered over, steamed in soup. The last leaf falls. He gets his rake.

After fifteen years, I came home. I came home, not from war, but from what looks like war. I'm the guy you might have been, but decided one day not to be. You get home and see the mess you've brought back. It begins to matter. This is the story of one man's mess.

I went over to get a closer look. I crouched down. The hole was in the concrete floor of the balcony. It was about two inches across and I could see right through to the parking lot below.

War will do things to your head. For instance, my name is Rob. I may, at times, resort to calling myself Rob. You can think of it as something I resort to. I'm not a retard, unless you consider the look inside a form. The sustained, sometimes unbroachable look. My story is a street corner. Today it is cold, so the story will be short. My hands are cold.

Like our computers, we are full of a nothing that demands substance. The substance we attain is nothing. Nothing remains. My trip away from home never happened. Those fifteen years? Never happened. And yet, I was away. And now I am back. And that's what this story is about. It's about being back.

You can't go home. I am home. You can't go home even when you are home. You're never home. When were you ever home? Home captured you one moment. Maybe when you were little. It got you. This idea of home. And now you know about it because you can't go there. It's that place you can't go to. You can almost go there. You get closest when you're furthest away. Like calculus. You get further and further close. The other side of the planet. The moon. Finally, the true reason for travelling to the moon. To go back home. To go back. Whatever is back. Maybe abuse is back. Maybe it's love. Maybe it's so much love it becomes abuse. You go back. Breaking free is considered something of an accomplishment. But then, accomplishment. Trap. You get the picture.

I was in Canadian Tire looking for garbage bags and at the same time — simultaneously, as they say — I was looking for the story of my return. Well, in actuality, I was looking for my *return*. Looking to *give* you the story. So, *actually*, there were three things. Me, what I wanted most, was *my* return. But I also wanted the story of my return, which, *ostensibly*, is for you, but it is really for me. All of it. *Also*, I wanted garbage bags. This most pressing. I had to get garbage bags. Line up at the checkout. Pay for the garbage bags. And get out of Canadian *Tire*.

Let's just be sure, okay. Let's just be sure of everything. Ask no questions. Make no excuses. We'll try to get to that point where you ask no questions (like that man on the corner asking his daughter, "Do you want to eat? I thought you wanted to eat. I don't need to eat. I thought you wanted to eat."). You don't want to be like that man. We'll try to get to the point where you aren't like that man. That will be the mission.

They went over to the park to have a picnic. Just the two of them. They took their pillows.
    They took the hibachi. They took the ketchup. The pickles. The relish. They took some dynamite. She took her sewing machine.

"Maybe I should take my table saw," he said.

"If you're taking your table saw, I'm taking my jewellery box."

"Why don't we just take the goddamn bed. I mean, if we're taking the pillows."

"What's wrong with taking the pillows? I thought you liked taking the pillows."

They put everything in the cooler. At the last minute, while she was freshening up, he slipped in a dildo.

He loaded everything in the car.

"Do you really think we should take our pillows?" she said. They were sitting in the car. She giggled. It was like they were going on a trip.

"Don't giggle," he said. He checked for traffic. Backed the car out of the driveway.

They drove the block and a half to the end of the street where the steel guardrail kept cars from driving into the park.

The park was crowded. It was beautiful. Families were there. Kids were throwing stale bread. Ducks. There were ducks everywhere. There was duck shit on the grass. There was no place to put the blanket.

"Here," she called. "Over here. This is a good spot."

He went over. Looked at the spot. He opened his mouth. Drew in a breath. He shook his head. He waved his hand over the grass. "Duck shit," he said.

She walked up the hill to the car to get a Kleenex.

They went over to the park to have a picnic. Just the two of them. They took their pillows.

They took the hibachi. They took the ketchup and the pickle relish. They took some dynamite. She took her sewing machine.

He said, "Maybe I should take my table saw."

"If you're taking your table saw, I'm taking my jewellery box."

"Why don't we just take the goddamn bed. I mean, if we're taking the pillows."

"What's wrong with taking the pillows? I thought you liked taking the pillows."

They put everything in the cooler. At the last minute, while she was freshening up, he slipped in a dildo.

He loaded everything into the car.

"Do you really think we should take our pillows?" she said when they were sitting in the car. She giggled. It was like they were going on a long trip.

"Don't giggle." He checked for traffic and backed the car out of the driveway.

They drove the block and a half to the end of the street where the steel guardrail kept cars from driving down into the park.

The park was crowded. It was a beautiful evening. Families were there. Kids were throwing stale bread. Ducks. There were ducks everywhere. There was duck shit on the grass. There was no place to put the blanket down.

"Here," she called. "Over here. This is a good spot."

He went over and looked at the spot. He opened his mouth and drew in a breath. He shook his head. He waved his hand over the area she had chosen. "Duck shit," he said.

She walked back up the hill to the car to get a Kleenex.

Makes me think of God. Of a bigger picture. The hands of God. Shaping the world. The world the story. But something falls. And now it is a very specific moment into which, because of my initial impulse, God is projected. God is trapped. Made to pay. Could be God lamenting the narrowness of the moment where we humans take his creation, his capacity for everything, and confine it to a moment, use a single moment to reinvent the capacity He thought only He contained. I don't know who Medea is. You could tell me if you like. Thanks for taking time to look at this.

I brought myself to climb the stairs to my mother's bedroom. Mother was dead.

"Are you dead?" I called.

Her eyes were open.

"You are dead, aren't you?"

One of her feet was sticking out from the covers. Her toes were purple. I wished she could have died with both feet covered. With her foot exposed, I felt like something was lost between us.

Something precious. Something that might have hovered between us, like a jewel in the air, if both her feet had been covered. I covered her foot and went out. One of her toenails was broken. *When did she break that toenail,* I thought. Meanwhile, the cancer was inside her body, eating her up. But I couldn't think when she would have broken that toenail. It must have been while I was with her. I might have been watching TV and she might have tried to get up. She might have tried to get up dozens of times. I might have been cooking eggs. There were things I could do. I could water the plants. Or just sit in the kitchen and think. There was no reason why I couldn't sit there and think. I don't think there was any reason. Sometimes it seemed like a good idea. Or I'd drink coffee.

When your mother wants to die at home, you have to call the police when it happens. I picked up the phone. The cord was frayed where it joined the receiver, and red and black wires were hanging out. I thought, "This phone won't last much longer. One day someone will pick it up and it won't work. The phone will have to be repaired, or a new phone will have to be bought." Then I thought, "So what? Say you have to buy a dozen new phones, each phone breaks and you find it can't be repaired, so you buy a new one. Say each phone costs a hundred bucks. So what?"

I called the police. The house was dark. There was one ray of light shining through the window above the front door. This one ray of light shone in like a spotlight in a dark theatre, and it struck one of the stairs on the staircase. I had to pass right through this ray of light to get to the kitchen, where I intended to make myself a good strong cup of coffee. This seemed like a wonderful idea, this cup of coffee, and all the way down the stairs I was so happy about this cup of coffee. I had decided to make a full pot so that I could offer a cup to the police officer when he arrived. I imagined he would be young with fresh skin, and sympathetic to my plight.

"Good morning," Jane mouths at the window.
"Good God," James says from the stairs.
Jane shakes her head.

Is it my fault the clouds look the way they look today?

I left the grocery store, my hands smelling of lettuce. I walked up the street. Ditches on both sides. I could walk to Tutti's house from work. I went up to where Tutti's old man's car was parked, hardly able to breathe. Tutti was at the door with that hair.

One of the things we had to worry about was putting our good clothes in the car without getting them wrinkled. Mom put them in a garment bag. Laid the garment bag down across the bottom of the trunk. She wanted to know if I thought they would be okay the way she had them, laid out across the bottom of the trunk like that. She shouted at me through the kitchen window. Told me to come outside and take a look.

"I'm trying to eat my dinner," I said out the window. I was wearing my slippers. She made me come outside in my slippers.

The first picture is on the first page. *Abacus*. Not a necessary choice. *Aardvark* precedes it. As does *aardwolf*. Animal illustrations seem to be a common choice.

There is no picture on the next two facing pages, although the opportunity exists in *Aberdeen Angus*, a breed of cow. A quick cross-reference shows that there is no illustration for *cow*.

The next two facing pages present little opportunity, however the editors have illustrated *abscissa*.

There are no more illustrations for four sets of facing pages.

Tutti is sitting beside me, sucking red licorice. The headlights from a car light up her face. Then darkness. Voices and shadows. Our voices. Our shadows.

The books come down a rubber ramp. They fall off the ramp into a big box on wheels. My job is to take them out of the box, look at the number on the spine, and, depending on the number, put them onto one of various shelves. I might put them into any one of a number of small boxes on the floor to my right. When one of the boxes gets full, I put it over by a certain table.

Eventually, somebody takes it away.

"Let her go," he mumbled to himself. "Just let her go." How to let her go, though. Get on the horn, maybe. Give someone a shout. Who to call was the thing, though. The thing he had to get just right, both the thinking it and the getting it, the getting being the who to call, just how in the hell to call.

I kept thinking, *So what?* It must have been a way of keeping sane. As soon as I stopped thinking, *So what?*, I cried. But for a while I would look at something. A worn spot on the carpet where the brown cord showed through. A chipped dish in the sink. I'd think, *So what?* This must have kept me from crying. But after a while I couldn't keep it up.

I don't even remember the guy's name. And Donna — I made that name up. Just to make things easier.
    If he went away for four days.
    I'd like it if…
    Well, first I'd have to have a husband.

Roy kicked the stone. Cars went by. Close. He watched the stone. Roy lived in a town. You could ride the bus to the city. There were still some fields. There was a cemetery. But no tombstones. The man in the suit stared into space. Eyes wide. He'd lost track. Of something. Last night a rainstorm. Knocked the leaves off the trees. The leaves were a different colour. The bus came. What could he do? Throw stones at people? He put money in the coin box. He was on his way to work. *I like where I work*, he told himself. *But not right now. Right now is a bad time. I have a lot to do.*

"That's kind of sad, when I know a song off by heart because you keep playing it. That means, Daddy, stop playing that song, because it's affecting your child's life."

We should have gone ahead and gotten a queen-sized in the first place. You see my line of reasoning? We should have got one with a lifetime warranty. What is killing us in this situation is that sometimes it's me he wants and sometimes it's his mother.

I go along the hall. The nightlight on in the socket over the counter. Trying to get all the way along the hall. Not waking anybody up.

What I can tell you is, and I don't mind saying this, I think I would be perfectly within my rights if I were to say it takes two to tango. Okay? This is not a one-way street we are barking up. This is not another person's tree. We are all of us in this house barking up the same tree with all of us to tango.

He gets down on the floor. He gets his blanket, his pillow, his Minnie Mouse dolly, and he gets down on the floor and lies there beside you. The truth is, if it were something you could go ahead and get away with doing, it would be a lot more comfortable on the floor than trying to get some sleep up there on the bed with him.

I'm not saying I don't like getting into bed with him. It's a matter of dimensions. We should have got a queen.

Bunk beds. We did consider bunk beds.

Okay, what if we had made a list? What if we had made a list of all possible things we wanted to consider? You know what? My list began and ended with bouncing. I thought I was doing pretty good considering the bouncing.

She says push him out of the way. She says that's what she does. She pushes him out of the way.

You could take next Friday off. Or all of the month of November. How would you decide, though?

What you could see out the window from there on the bed was a small, square section of the neighbour's roof and a short strip of sky. The plant in the middle of the windowsill was the one J had been clipping lately. The sprigs were in water glasses. Sitting in the kitchen. On the back of the stove. The section with the temperature dials on it. As soon as the sprigs grew roots, J transferred them into flower pots that she bought for five dollars each at the garden centre.

The girls want to know what kind of guy I am.

"I'm the kind of guy," I say. But that's it. That's all I say.

The girls laugh. Sit back against the wall. Turn their faces to the sun. "We're out here on our lunch hour getting tanned," one of the girls says. She looks at me. Her face is so close I can smell her tongue. "You could use some sun yourself," she says.

I looked at my watch. I read my book. I looked out the front of the bus. I looked at the side door of the bus. I watched a passenger get on the bus. I looked at my watch. I read my book.

I read my book. A passenger sneezed. I looked. The passenger sneezed. I looked at my watch. I looked at my knapsack. *I have what I have*, I thought. I looked out the front of the bus.

I looked at the side door. One passenger, I noticed, was eating potato chips. I could hear the potato chips. I could hear the bag crinkle when she put her hand in the bag of potato chips. I looked out the window. I looked at the cars out there. In the heat. *What could I have for dinner?* I thought. I watched a passenger get off the bus. I decided I would not go home.

I stepped off the bus. I looked up and down the road. The bus was gone. The sound of the bus was gone. I could hear my own breathing.

We put the kid in the buggy and rolled him down to the beach. I just wanted him to stop crying. *Stop crying*, I thought. *Go to sleep.* I wanted to go for a walk. But we couldn't go for a walk without taking the buggy. And you can't push a buggy on the beach. And anyway, I didn't want to go for a walk with the baby with us. I wanted to go for a walk like we used to go for a walk. Just us. And talking about things. The way we used to.

When she was pregnant, I got home from work before her every night and I threw my stuff down and got into some shorts and ran down the road to meet her. She walked home from work every day and I ran down the road to meet her and I could see her way down the road waddling toward me.

When I come home from work at night, she watches to see when I will fall asleep. She is waiting to see me fall asleep. It hasn't happened yet.

It happens just as you're about to leave. It comes upon you and it drains out of you. Swift. And silent. Or crippled and sudden. You have only that one moment trapped as it is. Trapped between the last moment and the next moments full of purpose. But in the brief in-between there's a moment of chance. That single slim hope.

"I'm warning you."
   "Don't warn me. I need no warning. I am a warning."
   He danced.

Don't get up unless you're willing to follow through. Stay. You've got your coffee.

I wanted to make things worse. I heard the knocking all the time now. The old man didn't look so old. His eyebrows were black. His eyes were green.

My wife is dead. I was out for a walk. I saw your house. I have children.

You should have found a better job. You should have gone to the counter one morning. Poured coffee. Sat. Washed the rain out of your hair.

There's a little boy next door. Comes out to his yard. Talks.

The old man moved his lips. "I have imaginary friends," he said. There was no one there to hear him.

The drugs may end your life, but your life will end. The drugs buy you precious luminous hours. Hours outside the dark mines of emptiness. They jerk your head back. Gaze you up.

You sat at the table. Lifted the spoonful of cereal. Milk dropped back to the bowl. Splattered small, almost invisible, drops across the table. You took no notice. Your eyes glazed. Your father said something. You were looking nowhere, into the world, into the nowhere into which you would move, into which your motionlessness would carry you, into which you would be carried. Carried away and then suddenly dropped.

"We have Internet now. That's it. There's nothing left to get."

"There'll be something else someday."

"Yeah. That's true."

"Will you get it?"

"I don't know what it is."

"Actually, there already is something else."

"What?"

"I don't know. I just heard about it. It's supposed to be really cool."

One morning, late in September, when the air was cold and the sun was a red blotch caught in a river of heavy cloud, Milly didn't climb onto the bus. Passengers were reading newspapers.

I was thinking. I was. I. Something. I was thinking something. The carpet. The red carpet.

It was how he came around the car that got up my ass.

"You want to drive?" he said.

"Sure," I said.

We were at a stoplight. He opened his door and got out of the car. When I realized what was happening, I grabbed the door handle on my side and tried to open the door without unlocking it.

You know that woman who cut her husband's dick off while he was sleeping? That's how I've gotten to feeling these days.

I finally got the door open and I went around the car as fast as I could. He was still standing by the driver's side door. He was butting out his cigarette with the toe of his boot. I got into the driver's seat just as the light turned green. He was coming around the front of the car with his ponytail behind him. I thought about running him over.

Near your turnoff, we passed an army truck sitting on the other side of the road with two army guys in the front. The army guys were smoking. You can take the front windshields out of those army trucks in case you have to shoot someone out the front of the truck. These two army guys had the front windshield out. And they were smoking.

The air conditioning came on. The people in the house woke up. It was the middle of winter. What was the air conditioning doing coming on?

I was the tinsel in the dried up needles of the Christmas tree.

Tutti came into the bedroom. "Act like a living entity for once," she said. I was on the bed. "Put on some underwear," she said. "Put on some socks. And a shirt. And some pants. You boor." It was spring. "We're going out for a walk. I have to go to the mall. I need buttons." She went out of the room.

I had to go on peoples' lawns to keep from getting a soaker. Every time there was less water on the sidewalk and I got back beside Tutti, Tutti licked her hand and reached over and tried to make some of the pieces of hair that were sticking up on my head go down. I sensed this was some kind of turning point. Tutti, I thought, might now be asking me to go walking places with her all the time.

Dad knew Terry Riley. Terry Riley didn't know Dad. Good. No one knew Dad. Dad played in his living room. He also played at the airport once a week. Dad sat at a piano off to the side while people lined up to buy plane tickets. But that wasn't the case at all. Dad only got to play piano when the regular piano guy was on break. His real instrument was sax.

One drunk guy named Billings was fat. He had fat hands. He shoved one fat hand out at Dad. The right hand. "Billings," he said.

"Dad," Dad said.

"Pardon?" Billings said.

"You said Billings. I said Dad."

"What does that mean?"

"I'm Dad."

"Not my dad."

"Call me Dad."

"Okay. I can do that. Dad."

"Great." Dad put his hand out. They shook. A plane pulled up behind Dad. The pilot looked in at Billings.

"Can you play a song for me? Dad."

"Are you drunk?"

"Play me a song. Play *Waterloo*."

"By Abba?"

"Yes. That's the one. Play *Waterloo* by Abba."

"I don't know any Abba."

"What kind of a piano player are you?" Billings asked.

"I'm not really a piano player," Dad said. "I'm a dad."

God doesn't matter one hoot beyond what he created when he created me. That's all. Thanks. Oh yeah, one other thing. God god god god god god god god.

"Isn't this great, Bob? This is a great place. God, I love this place."

The sun was shining. We were in this place for breakfast. The place had windows.

"I love breakfast. I love the breakfast menu. It feels greasy."

I had bacon and eggs. The waiter kept filling my cup with coffee.

"I love going out for breakfast. I love eggs."

The waiter splashed more coffee into my cup.

"I love coffee."

"This is good coffee." Bob took a sip of his coffee.

I took a sip of my coffee. We looked at each other over the edges of our cups.

"Where will you be going after this, Bob?"

"We haven't decided."

Bob was in New York with Bunny. Bunny is Bob's wife. Bunny was sitting next to me. Bunny and I were both sitting across from Bob. We were in an alcove by a window. The sun was in my eyes.

"Doesn't Bob have wonderful eyes, Bunny?" I looked at Bunny.

Bunny had wonderful eyes, too.

She put things on the bed. Stacks of clean underwear. They smelled from being outside on the line. She folded the underwear. Lay stacks of them on the spaces on the bed that were not covered by parts of my body or by pillows. She dumped stacks of ironing on the bed. Stood beside the bed ironing. Singing. She came into the room, closed the window, threw opened the curtains and ironed. This made my eyes hurt.

There's a moose down at the bank.

Are you comfortable? Do you want another chair?

It's not a real moose. It's a statue.

There are moose all over the city. It's a promotion.

A promotion for what?

I don't know.

For moose?

No. Not moose. Do you want a coffee?

No. I just had one before I came over here.

Why don't you eat that doughnut?

I'm on a diet.

You want to change tables? Is the sun in your eyes?

I like the sun.

In your eyes?

No. Just on me. It's not in my eyes.

This coffee tastes like shit.

This moose had jewels on it.

I heard Tom Cruise is in town.

Do you think he saw the moose?

I went in the washroom. Opened my book. Wrote: *I went in the washroom.* It was a fire alarm at work. A bell was ringing. The door on the washroom banged. I stopped writing. Closed the book.

We picked apples at the orchard. When we got home it was nice weather. I didn't think it would be a good idea for the boys to go in and play Nintendo. "Come and hit tennis balls against the school wall with me," I said.

Sammy hit a ball onto the school roof. Then I did. Shorty wanted to go home.

Later, when it was getting dark, I found a better wall. It was at the other school. It was a higher wall. And the roof was domed. The balls couldn't get stuck up there. I was alone this time. Hitting balls. I hit balls until it was too dark to see them. My back hurt.

At a certain time, on one particular day, I was just past the mall when I saw the stretch of my life wind out toward the edge where it writhed in its diminishment. I saw the severance. I understood the connection and the loss. I discovered the placement and the slot and I saw where the axe came down. I no longer had a life. I had a character.

The aim had been to chop things off as directly behind my life as possible, so I had this great weight of future pushing back on me with no past to fall into.

The snow shimmers down and down and down, settles first upon what it first settles upon, revising all upon which it settles.

I was in that place where I go which is a place which is only always not the place where I am, and no one telling me, *You are really here*. When it happens, it is me who says it. I say, *Here is where you actually are*, and then I can never come any further.

Sometimes it can last for days, but there is always that pinnacle, which is practically a hallucination, and then what is it but a redefinition of the same emptiness, a label that seems to tell you everything.

It's just a matter of getting to bed a little earlier every night.

Say it isn't healthy to sleep late, though. Say it.

I mean, really. Really. I mean.

I didn't really want to put the girls in here, because that would mean whole new characters to develop. But they kept going to get the phone. It was them who got the phone. I could have just left the phone out, but it kept ringing. I mean, even without the kids, there were interruptions.

I always loved Lewis. Remember seeing that movie? Where the house is full of boys? When I was pretty it was just a matter of thinking it was just the greatest. Everything was the greatest.

From that time on, I've loved Lewis. My father-in-law taped the door shut and would no longer come out. One for us. We pull it out now and then and watch it. Lewis has this oil slick in his back hairs when he's the cool guy. I thought he was pretty darn cool.

We were just at Jerry's and what a bed.

It must have been breathtaking, Lee.

Oh, it was pretty breathtaking, El. You know what I'm saying?

He spit through his teeth. PANIC.

Offstage: characters avoid them entirely.

Characters need to be played off against one another.

Reject the easiest thought.

They told me to get a voice. Take out the crap. Make it sparse. So I did it. I made things that were all voice.

Then they told me I needed a story. So I wrote these plots — beginning, middle, end — no characters. I lost my voice.

That's where I am right now. So…

"Life is iron ore," they told me. "Crush the iron ore."

"Life is generally boring," they told me, "with these moments of glory."

That's where they are. What do you think? Will they meet?

Sit down. Take a seat. Relax. Have a cookie. Have some coffee. Go upstairs. Walk the line. Name that tune. Bring a date. Buy a car. Eat me. Make it snappy. Wake the baby. Beat the band.

I don't know. It seemed we were drifting apart.

All at once, the lake dried up.

The end came too soon.

They told me to get a voice. So I went down to the corner where I know this guy, Johnny, who sells stuff.

"You got a voice?"

"I got a voice. You hear me talkin'?"

"You wanna sell it?"

"How much you gonna pay for it?"

We worked out a deal. I put the voice in my pocket. That left Johnny speechless.

I put the voice in my dog, Rex. Rex went down to the corner and sold stuff. I'm coming down the street and here I see Rex selling stuff he's taken from my apartment.

People hear my dog talking and they get excited. "Look at that — a talking dog."

I shrug.

"We could take it places. Show people. We could charge money."

I shrug again. *It's true*, I think, *we could charge money*.

There were four trees. They sat in the middle of a field. These funny little groups of people kept going by. In the last group, they all had hats. In another group that went by earlier, everyone was pushing a baby stroller.

"Who?" Tutti asks.

"Virginia Woolf. I'm reading this book by her," I say. I hold up the book. Tutti looks at it for a second. Then she goes back to doing crossword puzzles in the crossword puzzle book she bought in town today. She hates any crosswords where it takes more than a couple of seconds to get any of the words. She buys the jumbo crossword books that sell for eighty-nine cents each. These ones have the easiest crossword puzzles in them.

"Do you think I look good with a beard?" I say.

"What did you just say about Virginia Woolf?" Tutti asks. She's got the end of her pencil in her mouth and she is looking at me. She looks angry.

"I didn't say anything about Virginia Woolf," I say. "I said, Do you think I look good with a beard?"

"No," Tutti says, "before that. What did you say before that? About Virginia Woolf's ventricles?"

"I said," I say, "that I think Virginia Woolf has more ventricles than me."

"What the hell is that supposed to mean?" Tutti asks. "Everybody has the same number of ventricles."

"I know," I say. "It was a figure of speech," I say. "A way of expressing something I was trying to express."

"A way of expressing what?" Tutti says.

"I don't know, exactly," I say. "That's why I said it."

"If you don't know exactly what it is you were trying to say," Tutti says, "why were you saying anything?"

"I think Virginia Woolf is capable of a kind of writing I could never be capable of," I say. "That's what I was trying to say."

"Well, then why didn't you just say it?"

"I thought the thing of the ventricles was a better way of saying it. It was the thing that first popped into my head."

"Don't always say the first thing that pops into your head," Tutti says.

When we can't stand being on the campsite anymore, we go out driving. We drive into little towns and go into the grocery stores. Usually, Sammy falls asleep on these drives. While Sammy is sleeping, Tutti and I talk about what we will do on our vacation next year.

"I don't want to camp next year," Tutti says.

"Neither do I," I say.

"Maybe we should rent a cottage," Tutti says.

"You hate cottages," I say.

"I know," Tutti says.

Dear Will,

I write to you now out of a sense of declension. The verb falls, like the branch off an old tree, tipped away by the slightest breeze, ready to fall, but not falling. Then, finally, toppled by nothing.

There. I felt better. I went to the kitchen. Opened the fridge. Stood in its light. Closed the fridge. Went back to the living room. Sat. Stared. Truly, I felt better. Empty. Like the fridge. A little something here. A bag of milk askew on the bottom shelf. I'll be fine.

Dear Lou,

Another word arrives. Uninvited. Unacknowledged. Unrepentant. But it's not another word. At least, is it? It's the same word in a different suit. It went away to the change room briefly. Changed. Between sets. I mana your friend. I low to your gourd.

It was a horse-drawn woman. Or a horse-drawn horse. I wasn't sure. Mama took us to the beach that Sunday after church. Beautiful, dark-eyed, oblivious, fanatic, lofty, wind-blown Mama. She stood with her parasol resting on her shoulder, her skirts brushing the sand, fluttering in the breeze which skittered low, arriving from the south. The sky hung low over the horizon, but rose up directly above us like a sample of a blue ceiling. It was the mother of all ceilings, that sky. For it looked like the blue end of up. To the north, past the plastic likeness of a mallard that a cottager had settled over a rock cairn twenty feet from shore, you could see the nuclear station. A seagull caught my eye, wheeling black, then shiny, then gone against a cloud. The clouds were set across the sky like a squadron of bombers. Fat. With their bombs. Parked on a field. They hardly moved. And Mama hardly moved. Standing near where the waves stopped. Behind Mama, the little ones played in the sand.

Shortboy put his hands together and prayed. He was praying he'd get Amir. Amir wasn't even there. There was a guy who looked like Amir. But the guy had glasses. *Maybe Amir got glasses*, I thought. The guy was all the way across at the other end of the pool. *That's not Amir*, I thought. But I didn't say anything to Shortboy. *Let him pray*, I thought. *Let him have hope right up to the last minute.*

Another thing was, she wouldn't say one way or the other. You remember I had her at the beach and we were walking slow. She was walking slow. I was walking slow. I was only walking slow because she was walking slow. She wouldn't say.

"It's one way," I said. "Or the other."

But she wouldn't say.

"Let's go to the beach," I said.

"What time is it," she said.

"Ten-thirty, probably."

She didn't say anything. So we went to the beach.

When we got to the beach, she stood on the beach. With her shirt on. Near the water. I didn't say anything. I didn't want us starting in. We had this day off together. I wanted it to be nice. So I kept my mouth shut.

I swam and splashed and she stood outside the water. I swam and threw drops of water into the air with my hands in the dark air over the water even with the sun there in the blue sky and she stood there and I splashed and she came into the water. But she still didn't take her shirt off. It was like she was only half there. The bottom half. The half in her bathing suit. The other half of her was hanging around somewhere else, wearing a shirt.

When we got home, we went up to our apartment. We hung our wet bathing suits on the balcony to dry. Tutti walked around the apartment for a while, trying to solve some problem.

There was a baby and we lived in an apartment.

Tutti gets back from wherever she's been and I'm in the kitchen cleaning lettuce.

"What are you doing?"

"Cleaning lettuce." She can see that I'm cleaning lettuce. "I'm making a salad for you to take to work," I say.

"Thanks," she says. She goes into the living room.

I pack her salad in a plastic container. Put it in the fridge. I put salad dressing in a container. I put in a lot. Tutti says I never give her enough. I fill the container twice as full as I usually do. I put a lid on it. Put it in the fridge.

"Don't forget to take this with you." I stick my head around the corner into the living room. Tutti is doing push-ups.

I go in the living room. Lie on the couch. I realize I need to blow my nose. I get up and go and do that. I come back. Lie down on the couch. I go to sleep.

I wake up. Tutti is cleaning.

"You know you make little noises when you're going to sleep."

"I know." I know because I've woken myself up with those little noises. I wake up and I know I've made some sort of funny little sound. The other night I woke up and I knew that I'd let out a little laugh. I wondered if Tutti heard it. I wondered if she was awake.

"Are you asleep?"

"Maybe."

"Did I just make a little noise?"

"Yes."

"I know." And I did know. I didn't need to ask. I wanted to know if she'd heard it. "I was laughing."

"It didn't sound like a laugh."

"I was laughing in my dream. I can't remember what I was laughing at."

Sometimes I stop breathing just before I go to sleep. I make a gasping noise. Or sometimes I get frightened and let out a scream. I don't think it comes out as a scream, though. It's like I want to scream, but something inside me stops me.

I get off the couch. Go for the vacuum cleaner. What bothers me right now is the look on Tutti's face. She gets that look whenever she's cleaning. It's her worst look. I can't even describe it.

Tutti pulls all the cookbooks off the counter in the kitchen. There are crumbs back there. Tutti looks pissed off. She isn't, though. That's just it. Maybe she is, maybe she isn't. You can't tell. That vacant look leaves too much to the imagination. One thing you can be sure of: she isn't happy.

She cleans the counter while I do the vacuuming. Pretty soon it's time for her to drive me to work. "I love a clean place," she says. "Don't you?"

"I do," I say.

She looks so happy. She's got her salad packed in her gym bag.

There was one car moving slower than the rest. That's the advantage of living on the thirty-first floor. The car kept moving slower and other cars sped by. The highway was raised and the city sat below it, but from the thirty-first floor it was all one level, and the headlights whizzed by the one set of headlights that was hardly moving now until it finally just stopped. Didn't veer, or get off the road or out of the lane, or edge over at all, just slowed and slowed and stopped and the other cars whizzed by going places that I couldn't see even from the thirty-first floor.

What I like about it is that it attempts to be a rational, all-encompassing system explaining the relationship between God and man, yet it always seems slightly unconnected to anything you or I might consider rational, and in places it diverges rabidly away from anything remotely rational. It's a real critique of rationality without trying to be, because it shows how any rational system might be compelling, in a way astrology never seems able to manage.

They wanted to kill their cats.

My wife had poison oak.

She was watching *Beverly Hills 90210*.

She had socks on her hands.

God goes into the grocery store. He picks up a head of lettuce. Puts it back. Too expensive. The mystery of His ways cannot account for the price of lettuce this week. The sky, a weave of jet-stream clouds God traverses on his way home from the grocery

103

store. *Is this my doing?* God is thinking. *I can't remember what I was thinking when I started this thing. I am four billion children away from the purity of my origins. What was the deal, anyway? Was I supposed to be accountable for clouds I didn't create? Or was I going to let the bastards fry in their own oil?*

The boss came running out across the flat brunt of the quarry and called up to me saying he had a job for me and that I was to hightail it over to the box immediately. So I fired up the angel and hightailed it over to the box. But then I got to pondering, on the way to the box, all the lunches I'd cut short because of the boss coming running across the brunt of the quarry, so when I got the angel down into the box, I parked her there and left her idling. I put my feet up. I was tired. Tired of the job, tired of the bitch I was married to. I went to sleep.

When I woke, I could hear the boss's voice hollering down from the brink. I looked up over the shovel and saw him there. There he was. Running down the slope into the box. I kicked the angel into gear and rumbled toward the boss and when I got to where he was, I kept going.

The new *Roget's Thesaurus* is out. Have you seen it? I got mine yesterday. It is a sight to behold. It truly is. You will have to see it for yourself. I don't think there are words to describe it. I'll bring my copy down to show you on the weekend if I have room in my suitcase.

Are you all right down there? You can be honest with me. I worry about you down there, all by yourself. I wish I could get down there more often to see you.

The guys up here laugh when I show them my new *Roget's Thesaurus*. Whenever I read one of my stories, they always say, "You didn't write that. Roget did." Only they say Row-jet. That's how they say Roget. They say, "You didn't write that, Martin. That was written by Row-jet." Can you imagine? These are the people I have to spend my days with. These guys call themselves writers.

I'll tell you something. They all wear hunting jackets up here.

And some of them bring their guns into the cafeteria with them at lunch. They want to be able to jump right up in the middle of lunch and run out into the compound and blow the head off any poor animal that happens to stray into the compound by accident. Can you imagine? These are the guys I spend my days with. These guys call themselves writers. I wouldn't call them writers. I know what I would call them, and it wouldn't be writers. And it wouldn't be something they list in *Roget's*.

You know what? I'm going to bring my new *Roget's* down for you for sure. Hang it. I'll just bring less clothes is all. I don't need a whole lot of clothes when I'm down there anyway. What do I need a whole lot of clothes for?

If there is anything you need down there, you make sure and let me know. I know it must be lonely for you down there. You know what? If you want a *Roget's Thesaurus* of your own, I'll get you one. Okay? Hang the expense. Because I'll just go out and get you one, no questions asked, and it's on me. Hang the expense.

Everyone in our neighbourhood can see everyone else through their kitchen window.

By choice, and by being a wise man, he would not be able to put his pants on right. Anyone who had three feet on his head and, furthermore, had them there because he wanted them there, was a very sick individual, one most likely devoid entirely of reason. This, in the end, was what was most disturbing.

It hit Tutti the hardest. Tutti did most of the crying. She couldn't make a sandwich without crying. She would go into the bathroom and turn on the water so I couldn't hear her sob. One time, she turned on the hair dryer even though I knew her hair was already dry.

I was afraid to call my mother. I didn't know what I'd say. I sat by the phone for a while. Then, instead of phoning Mom, I went to get the mail. There was a letter from Grandpa. I read half of it, but then I had to stop.

Cye's mother died. Cye started coming into work wearing her mother's clothes. She talked about dreams she had where her mother phoned her up and complained about all the pain she was having. She complained about the weather and about her son, Cye's brother. Cye's brother was also dead. After a few weeks, Cye started making jokes about her mother calling her from a pay phone in heaven, with her brother standing outside the phone booth under a big dark sky with lots of stars and a convenience store on the other side of the parking lot.

Cye had her Master's degree, but she couldn't land a full-time position. She moved from one temporary job to another, talking about her dead mother's library card, which she kept meaning to have purged from the system, but which she kept leaving in her other purse.

Saturdays were strange days because there were no managers in and doughnuts were provided. Louella wore white shorts and pink or blue t-shirts and blue underwear which could be seen through her shorts. She moved around fast and sat down as often as possible.

"I should do some womanly chores soon," Tutti says.

I have to laugh.

"Clean out the fridge," she says. "Clean all the utilities."

"What utilities?" I ask.

She ignores me. Goes on rambling. She gets her big blue bag. Starts taking things out. Bits of paper. Empty gum wrappers. "I should look at my schedule," she says. "So I know when I have time to do my womanly chores."

He's always at the edge of something he doesn't understand. The other day I found him standing over the toilet in the little bathroom on the main floor. He was holding an adjustable wrench. A big silver one. He didn't seem to see me watching him. He tapped the wrench in his empty hand. The mirror behind him. Reflecting the back of his head.

The actual Harrison Ford sailed a boat up a river and walked for a time until the insects got to him and he stopped and built a house. Other Fords later joined him and eventually a grocery store opened.

Whether or not Ken believed in God is a matter scholars have debated endlessly.

God, in one form or another, has been around for a long time. Born of Jewish parents in a ghetto in the homeland, God saw, when he was a first-year university student, the potential of dividing the land from the sea and the air and also the importance of light and The Word.

It's a long story, but one I think you'll find worthwhile if you just keep reading.

Fluffy is eighteen. She can't hear anymore. One of my friends calls her dead-ears. My sister had a cat. Truly, it was called. Truly is dead now. Truly and Fluffy. Sisters. The guy who gave us Truly named her Truly. He worked in a movie theatre. Truly was the name of a character in a movie. I'm the one who named Fluffy Fluffy.

Just keep reading.

Tutti sews. I watch a movie. I've got a cup of coffee. Tutti thinks we should get a petition going.

"There have been plenty of petitions," I say.

"That's true," she says. We go out on the balcony. The sun breaks free of the clouds.

"How about politics?" I say. I go back into the apartment to get my coffee. Tutti follows me. Goes back to sewing. The movie is almost ending. Women in grey uniforms are running out of an institution. Charlie Sheen had to get the Senator's daughter out. He loves her. Charlie and the Senator's daughter cross a river.

"I want to save the world through politics," Charlie says.

"That's a laugh," the girl says. She says all she knows about politics is that you have to smile at people you don't like.

"First you have to take care of yourself," Tutti says.

"What's that supposed to mean?" I ask.

"Just what I said."

"I take care of myself."

"Then I make something," Jane says. "I hate it."

"I don't want to see the caboose," James says. "I turn and run into the forest. I hear the train. I know when it's gone. A million years have passed."

The wind dies. He's not sure what to think about. He keeps looking at the place he was looking at all along. Nothing has changed.

I hate the orchestral arrangement, but I dearly love the musicians, each afraid to play beyond what I love. It's what did all that killing in '88 and again in '97. That and the earthquake.

Did you notice his hair is pretty messy? Jet black. His eyes are black, too. His red sweater is black, too.

The boy sleeps and I read *Bambi*. The boy fell asleep. I was falling asleep. The woman came in. "Are you staying in here?" the woman asked. Somehow I thought I would stay in there. It would make more sense. *Stay in the boy's room*, I thought. *Sleep*. I would have slept in there.

The sundae that I would like to eat would be the level 2 sundae. I would want to eat the level 2 sundae because I wouldn't want to get too fat on the level 4 sundae and there's a banana in the level 3 sundae and the level 1 sundae wouldn't fill me up. That's why I would eat the level 2.

I was in the aisle where the things I saw made me think of garbage bags. My heart beat. I would soon find the garbage bags. Almost as though finding garbage bags could be enough. The obvious question: Were the garbage bags the same as the story of my return?

A pizza commercial comes on the radio. Tutti dances around the room. Cleans more stuff. Takes stuff out of her bag: staples; an apple; some clothes; underwear.

He was thirty-seven years old. The cottage was his. He opened his eyes. He had a feeling. It wasn't a good feeling. It was 5:30 in the morning. It wasn't the feeling he'd hoped for. He tied his tie four times. Drove slow.

He took his shoes off. Rolled up his cuffs. He was afraid to turn around. Finally, he turned around. It was beautiful to turn around.

A week passed. They would never see Milly again.

We have our secrets. We distribute them accordingly. We have the capability. Security can be at risk. Security must not be breached.

Who will lead us to salvation? Anyone? Somehow I doubt it.
What about an ongoing awareness session?

We could go out. On a day-by-day basis. There's been some discussion, right? Is this the right approach? Christ, we wasted time. We found new and incredibly innovative ways to waste our time. Then, they paid us back. They talked and they wouldn't stop talking. So what do you do in a case like that? You kill them. You fucking kill them. Dead. That will shut them up. Yet, they are so nice when they aren't talking.

Hello, my name was Charlie. But I had to get glasses and it was Melody's fault. Melody was beautiful. But it hurts. I wear hats like you've never seen. Good night, Mel, she said. I was alone in a room.

In a room alone, they feed you. They give you water. You could wash. But you could not speak. You had no one to speak to. No one to touch. So what do you think happens to you? Go ahead. Use your imagination. Don't be afraid. Speak your mind. No one cares. You can say anything. No one is even listening. Even if you get a single word just right. A single word dropped into the single right space. The single right word dropped between the right two silences.

Too many words, Meg.
　　Don't die on me, Ronnie.

How perfect could it be?

Shit, I've got a hole in my chin. I need sleep. I need to investigate the possibilities.
　　No, Cindy, you can't investigate everything.
　　You can investigate for the rest of your life. Eventually you have to step out. Out of your pants. Out of your skin. You won't die. You might die. You will die. Eventually. Die. Okay. Die now. Get it over with.

Goldie? God. Who was it? Who is it? Where are they? On the phone?

Get your briefs lower down, Kate. Will you give me love? Will you give me God? Will you give me a comprehensive list? What will you give me, God? Kate? Will you give me funding? Will you fund my project? Get chilled, Charlie. Get God. Get Gill. Get fucked. Get sun. Get small. Get heavy. Get leery. The black blank sun of god. There was no other way. I helped shine the green. Renew the western hills, Caroline. Get ye to a haberdashery. Glow on nor we fly. God is next to cleanliness. Holy cows. Mid-sized cars. Little brains. Do a fucking meeting. Big ideas. Workbooks. The hearts of staff today. The long fields we walk in. Let us know what you think. Hate us. Love us. Don't care. You suck. You rock. Don't snore, Daddy. Snore. Don't whisper words.

What I do when I'm feeling sad or alone is I have this pool of hate in my stomach, like a little pool of acid, and I try to feel the depth of that pool. I swim down and try to touch bottom and still know I can make it back up without running out of breath. It's impossibly deep, you know.

Got a knife? Or an axe? Bring it. Bring it out into the street with you today. Run with it in the wind. Run with your long hair behind you and your axe out front in the wind, brother. Kill something.

It's so cold today. The wind bites off my nuts. Bits of snowflake, like something shaved off God's beard. God's breath. So cold.

She died. Gone. Where is she now? Have a piece of snow, Little One. Have some cake.

I made a problem. Look!
  She dances. Hearts continue to beat. Harmony, my love. We miss each others' notes. We sing our separate songs. We hear each other sing. Placate those who are not prepared to sing. Sing quietly in your head. Kill those who sing without hitting any note at all. We are, in our notes, naked, hair on our asses, deep inside our pardons.

And to think of the many testicles and toasters we have smitten. There's an engine, they say. (Clear your throat, darling.) *A-hem.* At the end of the day, type in the colour of your coat. Watch what happens then. It will fundamentally change everything. It should make things more simple.

We were trying to get up the hill. Finally, I gave up. *Fuck it,* I thought. I turned to go back home. I glanced over my shoulder. The hill was gone.

Yes, technology this and technology that.

Finally, we slept.

His talent was he could hold his breath underwater for a long time. *I don't want to hold my breath any longer,* he said when he was nine years old. He gave up holding his breath.

The ominous news for book fans is relentless.

Kiss me here, dear. Then go to your book club. I'll be all right. I'll be sitting here, right here, when you get home. Wear your red coat. It is cold out there today. But you will be beautiful.

She was disappearing into her face. It was the strangest thing. If I glanced at her in passing, I could barely see her in there. I could hear her when she talked, like someone trapped inside a closet. Like she was trapped inside her clothes. Her makeup. But the harder I tried to look for her inside her eyes, the smaller her eyes seemed to get.

There comes a time when words break free of the world and ballast themselves, seeking other words to cling to and ward off. When this happens, each word is lost as soon as it passes. But this is always the way with words. When the words break free, however, they leave nothing behind, seek nothing and kindle nothing. These words leave the world to be what it already was. They stand beyond, but parallel to the world, for they come themselves as absolute being. At this point, there can be no love, no hate, no attachment, no nothing. Just wonder, like the open mouth of the wind, felt by all, yet subject to none.

I wanted to put my thumbs on her eyelids and rub her makeup off. But I didn't have to. She was crying so hard, her makeup was running all down her face, and suddenly I could see her. I could see how hot those tears must feel. They were mine.

The fuckers wanted *Broken Hearted Melody*. So I played it. And I broke all their fucking hearts. Then I put all my music in my music satchel, stuffed the satchel under my arm, picked up my instrument case, and walked out of there like I was never coming back.

Last time I saw Heather, she was patting the sheep. I hated that sheep.

Onward, they say. But hither too? Wither? Blither? De dither. Wither de dither de blither.

I was going to call the book *Emma's Head*. Emma could tip her head back so you could see down her neck. There were lights in there and translucent bits of something floating around that looked like little fly wings moving in a gentle wind. It was weird. I couldn't do a whole book though. Every time I looked down Emma's neck it was different. But it was something different in my head, not in Emma's neck. I saw in the light and the fly wings something different. Not like something you could describe in words. Not like where you'd have a whole book with chapters and a table of contents and stuff. It was going to be non-fiction.

Brown eyes. She had brown eyes. She smudged her lipstick on mirrors in public bathrooms with her thumb so people thought she was kissing mirrors.

TO DO LIST:
- kill Bowser
- read more books
- do laundry
- eat food from other countries

I never pretended to be smart. I don't know what I've done. I never pretended I wouldn't hurt. I don't try to hurt. I don't pretend to know. I am not afraid. I am not afraid of anything. I don't pretend to know everything. I'm not afraid of what I don't know about. Why would I ever love anything I knew everything about. Why would I be stupid enough to believe I know everything about anything.

I'm reduced to something so raw, it hurts to walk. I have made me like this. I see that the me that made me like this can pull me back out, and the me that pulls me back out can make me stumble and crawl. I walk and I almost stop. I speak and I move again. I want to fall and fall and stop and be held. I don't care if I feel frantic or happy or savage. I just want to lie safe somewhere and die safe there for a while and stop being alone, speaking such loneliness as words always speak. I want to speak wounds and feel them on my tongue.

What might disgust you about me — Jesus, what already has disgusted you about me — is the way I give up and act like I have no choice. You see that in me? You tell me to smarten up. That's a very beautiful thing to do for me. You don't have to do that. You make the choice to do that.

I went in the bathroom here and cried. Then I worked on my library work and tried to make my music loud enough to hurt my ears. Then I went in the bathroom and kicked the wall a few times and cursed myself. Then I went outside and walked in the cold rain. I laughed out of control at Roger, my friend who lives outside the doughnut shop, when he told me the cops come by all the time and write down what he's wearing so they'll know who he is if they find him dead in an alley in a couple days from now.

I can't promise you anything. I don't know why I would ever want to shut you up again, but apparently I'm an asshole.

I was born in Amsterdam and our mother put me in a basket at birth and put me in one of your canals and I floated to Canada and was adopted.

 I like that room. There's a big window, almost across the entire wall, and some trees and the townhouses across the road and behind them huge trees poking up from the ravine with a little river in it. When I was a boy, the place where I lived was a cornfield and I used to walk along beside the little river to get to school.

I feel like I just got fucked by someone immortal, someone who has no right to fuck a human being. I can't breathe.

When God died, he became a man. When someone wrote a history of Jesus, he became a man. Thus, what kills us is always another man. Someone is going to kill you and you don't know who it is. You can try to protect yourself, but the enemy is all around you if that's the road you choose. Or you can stop being afraid. It's up to you.

"Everything fell apart," a man said.

God glanced down. Shook his head. *When was everything ever together?* He wondered. He seemed about to cry.

It would rain later. People in gray coats. Lined up. Standing in puddles. Waiting.

What are they waiting for? God thought. He pulled out his handkerchief. Dabbed beneath his eyes. God has no eyes, though. But he could imagine having eyes. He could imagine this so clearly. He could put his handkerchief beneath his eyes and almost feel them there.

There's so much to be sorry for, God thought. He touched his chin. He could almost feel a chin where his chin would have been if he had ever had a chin. *I'd have whiskers,* God thought. It made him smile to think like this. *I'd shave every morning. I'd have a briefcase.*

Dee-de-dee-deet-deet. Newsflash. Grey sweaters are no longer available. Except at certain locations. Look at the veins in my arm. I look at them. They look blue. Beautiful. Like rivers. Like a map of rivers. Mapped. Something made by satellite. Forgotten for a hundred years. Then found in cabinet in a little corner office in an abandoned building on the other side of town from the side where the men in brown coats laugh and wait to die in a bar with nothing much in it. A once-beautiful woman serving drinks. Laughing at some things the old men are saying. Not hearing most of what gets said. Hearing mostly a voice in her head talking about a husband and children she may never have had. Each evening, on her walk home, going past the fires in oil drums and the men sleeping in doorways, she wonders: *Will the children be there? And what of Lance?*

Everything I ever wrote was a way to try to trick myself into seeing myself arrive suddenly and unexpected with a secret message of love. But it isn't possible, of course. So I need some-one else. Anyone interested? You see, I've tried to give away what I have and no one wants it. No one wants my gift. That's the sudden surprise that will take your breath away — someone will-ing to take you as a gift and not deconstruct you, but just say, *Thank you. Thank you for all of you, not this or that little piece of you, but just all of you, Ken Sparling, all of you at once and no question about how you are made up of a bunch of little pieces.*

I wanted Mark to get his PJs on and brush his teeth and I wanted Deve to turn his light out and go to sleep, but you can't make a person. You can, but at what cost. At what cost do you gain that control. Oh, I don't care, really. Fuck it. I need to go to sleep. I need her to touch me out of a desire for me. I should just give up. It isn't ever going to happen. I haven't given up, though. I'll wait. I hope, still. I am naïve. I want to be just that naïve.

Sometimes when you take the coffee filter out, you get two by mistake and you have to stuff the extra one back in the bag. Then, later, when you go to use the one you stuffed back in the bag, it's crumpled up and it's harder to get it to sit in the basket right. You risk the danger of getting coffee grounds in your coffee.

Come where you is till I get where you're at.

Every morning you sit at the head of the day and the things in the day that the day comes to bring toward you. It might be kids. It might be pimples. It might be death. Everyday it could be death that comes toward you and you have to ask yourself, *What do I do today until death gets here? Do I sit here and wait for it? Or do I ride out to meet it?* You would think, *Ride out and meet it,* is the right answer, wouldn't you? But there is no right answer. There is only an answer. And then some other questions.

I've been at the library for nearly twenty years. I don't give a fuck about it, really. On days like yesterday, it seems like the most horrible place in the world. Today, I know it will be as beautiful as everything else I set eyes on. So, I don't really consider another job. Another job would be the same as this fucking job.

In the days that followed, the dirty men grew bold. They left their rubber boots on the porch. Sat at the kitchen table. Ate. Meanwhile, mothers all over the neighbourhood tried to reason with their children. Many dirty men walked on the sidewalk. Marilee's mother seemed preoccupied. Marilee tried to see the men's faces. Marilee's grandmother baked a pie. She took Marilee into the garden. She said nothing. But she nodded. As though she had heard someone speak and she was listening.

"They are under the palm trees, Grandmother," Marilee said. "They love no one and no one loves them."

I came from this weird place and it looks funny. I like the place I came from. It's fun! I like those silver and gold circles you call money.

I went up this thing that moved. I went into the thing. I looked over the side of the huge thing that I was on and something almost came out of my mouth! You should try it, it's fun!

Then I spread out the wings I got from Toys-'R'-Us (whatever that is). I looked on the side of them and it said, "Caution, not for skydiving," then, just that second, I landed on some white fluffy things. I think they were in a truck. (I know that much about your planet.) I ended up getting kicked out and back into my pile of mush. I got two of those white fluffy things. They're fun!

KEN SPARLING works for the Toronto Public Library system. He lives with his wife and two sons in Richmond Hill, Ontario, and rides his bike into downtown Toronto each day in all seasons. He is the author of [A Novel by Ken Sparling] (Pedlar Press, 2003), and *Dad Says He Saw You At The Mall* (Knopf, New York, 1996).